Into The Light

Into The Light copyright © Alys Hall

Cover design by Elena Tarsuis

ISBN 978-1-7395845-3-5

Barnard Publishing

Mold, Wales

barnard.publishing@gmail.com

www.barnardpublishing.co.uk

The Mabinogion are a collection of Welsh tales that stretch back as far as the 12th century, though they go back much further in the oral tradition. They have traditionally been presented as four 'branches' following Pwyll, Branwen, Manawydan and Math. The tale of Culhwch and Olwen is an Arthurian tale, but it is often included with the Mabinogion in many collections of the tales. The tales take their readers through heroic quests, war, deception, the complexities of love and much more.

I grew up with these tales at home and in school. I didn't notice it at the time, but there was something big missing from them. They were largely male-focused and, when the woman appeared (if at all), they were only there to enrich the man's journey. When I reflected on this, I felt that the woman's voice was left in the shadows or, worse, ignored completely. I decided that I wanted to retell these tales, but with some contemporary twists. I have largely focused on the women who appear in the tales and used the foundations of the originals to create something new.

To those who have never come across the Mabinogi before, I would like to remind you that this is a retelling and not every aspect of the stories are accurate to the original. And to those who already know them, I hope you might be able to open yourselves to this reinterpretation and enjoy these wonderful tales in a completely different light.

~Alys

"Yes, that is correct."

"You are not curious to know who I am?" Pwyll raised his head.

"I know who you are. You are Pwyll, Prince of Dyfed. I have seen you many times at court," Rhiannon said. His predictability, she thought, was somewhat comforting.

Pwyll tugged the reins of his horse and his chest rose. He seemed glad that she knew who he was. Rhiannon led her mare to the stream and let her drink with Pwyll's horse. She dismounted and Pwyll did the same. Patting her mare, she waited for his next words.

"I am here to ask for your hand in marriage, fair Rhiannon," said Pwyll. "You are, quite simply, the most beautiful woman to have graced this earth."

Rhiannon's eyes danced. She raised them to Pwyll and found that he had, in the blink of an eye, knelt on one knee. He held out his hands and Rhiannon took them. His hands were soft and sweating profusely. The man was completely at her mercy and she could not have believed her luck.

"How convenient. I was hoping that you would do exactly that. I am currently betrothed to Gwawl ap Clud and would be grateful to be rid of him," Rhiannon explained. "My father promised my hand to him in exchange for money, but unfortunately the man is insufferable and not likely to die anytime soon."

Pwyll's eyes widened. How had he not caught wind of this arrangement? He knew he had to set about breaking off their engagement as soon as possible. If anyone would marry Rhiannon, it would be him and him alone. His mind was already working at what scheme he could devise to break off whatever arrangements had already been made for them.

"I will speak to your father," Pwyll said. "He may have all Dyfed's riches if he so wishes, as long as I have your hand in marriage."

Pwyll rose from his knee and suddenly bent his head to kiss Rhiannon. Stunned, she stood there and received his kiss without a single movement. He broke away and, blushing, knelt on his knee again. Rhiannon looked down at the man and wondered what her Alaw would say to this.

Days later, Rhiannon found herself walking a familiar trail to where the water lilies floated in clusters along the freshwater ponds. Her steps to Alaw felt heavier today than they had ever done before. Telling her the news about her betrothal to Gwawl was punishing enough, but relaying the news about her engagement to the Prince of Dyfed would break Rhiannon's heart.

Alaw lay lounging around near the bank of a river. The water nymph was completely naked and basking in the sunlight with a cluster of bluebells growing beside her. A full basket of flowers sat on her right side and she would routinely take them out and smell them. It was Rhiannon's basket and it was regularly filled with nature's riches for Alaw to treasure and use.

Rhiannon lay beside Alaw and gently kissed her neck. Alaw turned to face her lover with tears in her eyes. Water poured from her lids like the river beside them and Rhiannon found herself licking the freshwater tears away. She moved her lips from her tears to kiss her but Alaw pulled away.

"I know about Pwyll if that's why you're here," Alaw said.

Rhiannon sighed. The forest seemed to hold all the secrets she possessed. What was the use hiding the truth? The trees were all-seeing and all-hearing and she was powerless to keep anything away from them. Rhiannon tried to console her and kiss her again, but Alaw, defiant, rose to her feet. She tried to wipe away the tears from flowing along her face but found that they refused to stop flowing.

"It changes nothing between us," Rhiannon said. "I will always love you no matter what occurs outside of us."

"It changes everything," Alaw snapped. "You would hurt me like this again? And what about Gwawl?"

"He is better than Gwawl. He is kind and will understand that I need my freedom," Rhiannon said. "I need my freedom to be with you."

"And what then? You will come to me whenever things with him are getting difficult?" Alaw sneered. "I refuse to be used, Rhiannon. I deserve better than that."

"You deserve the world and more," Rhiannon said. "I vowed to you that I would give myself over to you fully and that is a vow stronger than any mortal bond."

"If you kept to that vow, you wouldn't even be entertaining the idea," Alaw said.

Alaw placed her legs into the river and readied herself to sink deep into its depths. Rhiannon grasped onto her arm and tears began to spill from her own eyes. She could not bear to see the love of her life leave like this. If she were not at the behest of her father Hefeydd Hên, Rhiannon would have joined her by now. She was a half goddess and it was the mortal half which prevented her from living as she wished.

"I come to you as I am, in my joy as well as my sorrow. I cannot stand it, Alaw, as much as you cannot," Rhiannon cried. "Do you think I want this? Do you think I have a say in any of this, really?"

"Do what you need to do, but do not come back to me," Alaw snapped before submerging herself in the river.

Rhiannon watched her swim further and further away and she collapsed onto her knees in grief. She sobbed into the ground where Alaw lay and felt her body begin to shake in spasms. Rhiannon pressed the palm of her hand into her heart and shrieked into the dirt. She sat there for hours calling Alaw's name but no answer came from the water.

When she returned to her father's castle, she was inconsolable. Rhiannon refused to speak to anyone for days and the feast where she would take Pwyll's hand was fast approaching. Her father had already accepted Pwyll's offer and their betrothal would be announced before the court. Pwyll warned her that there may well be a competition of sorts to win her hand between himself and Gwawl ap Clud. Rhiannon couldn't have been any more indifferent about the whole affair. Pwyll assumed that her sorrow came from what would certainly be a duel with Gwawl on the day of the feast.

When the day arrived, Rhiannon stared blankly into the mirror as the maids prepared her. They braided her hair and she stared deeply into her own eyes. Her eyes had not danced since Alaw left her and she doubted that they would dance again. They had become rock solid and dark circles were forming under her eyes. She felt her tears threatening to fall but they were always hanging on the edges of her lids. Rhiannon wondered whether there was any warmth left inside of her.

She returned every day to the same spot where Alaw left her but the nymph was nowhere to be found. She might have been swimming deep into the waters and refusing to emerge until she was certain that Rhiannon was gone. Alaw might have left for other waters to stop the pain of all the happy memories they shared in that very spot. Her heart broke every time she found the riverbank empty.

The maids took their turns to prepare her and Rhiannon closed her eyes. She could not bear to look at her own reflection and what had become of her. What use was being a demigoddess if she could not use her power? The side of her that was mortal was tying her down and she wanted to be rid of it. She wanted to be with her Alaw. She wanted to listen to the rhythm of her own heart and follow it. She knew, however, that her father would certainly kill her or, worse, kill Alaw for all that had transpired between them.

The feast was prepared and the guests were welcomed into the hall. Rhiannon was the last to arrive and she drew the eyes of those already seated. She took a seat and tried to avoid Gwawl and Pwyll's searching eyes. She sat with the other ladies and made what polite conversation she could manage with them. She wanted to be anywhere but here in this hall. She would forever continue to grieve for her loss and wondered whether the shards of her heart could ever reassemble back into place.

Once the feast finished, the dancing commenced. Gwawl made his way over to Rhiannon immediately and grasped onto her arm. She spun and stared deep into his enraged eyes.

"You are betrothed to Pwyll?" Gwawl spat.

"Yes, I am," Rhiannon replied.

"Your father promised your hand to me," he hissed.

"Well, he has changed his mind. My father is a changeable man. Now, if you will excuse me – " Rhiannon started.

"No, this will not go ahead. I will fight for your hand in a duel," Gwawl muttered under his breath before he dropped Rhiannon's arm and turned to find her father.

Again, predictable, she thought. Rhiannon sighed and pointed to where her father sat on the table. Hefeydd Hên was laughing with Pwyll until they saw Gwawl storming along the hall to speak with them. Had Pwyll not been Prince of Dyfed, Gwawl would likely have taken out a sword and killed the man where he stood. Instead, he would be required to follow the rules of a duel and earn Rhiannon's hand. She watched their heated discussion from afar. Gwawl pointed at her every so often and she dropped her eyes to the floor. They were bartering her and she could not stop it. She yearned, more than anything, to return to the place where the water lilies swam on the pond.

~

The duel would take place outside and Rhiannon would stand, like a prize, beside her father. They readied themselves with their weapons and it only struck Rhiannon in that moment that one of them may well die fighting for her. She knew little about duels and simply wished to disappear. In her heart, she did not want either man to win. Alaw was planted firmly in her mind and she would have given the world and more to have her as a wife.

When the duel commenced, the crowd erupted into yells. Rhiannon watched Pwyll and Gwawl fight with their swords. It was clear, from the crowd's reaction, that they wanted their Prince to win. Rhiannon doubted that anyone supporting Gwawl would be left unharmed. She watched as Pwyll gained the upper hand and got him firmly onto the floor. Gwawl held up his hands in surrender and Pwyll pointed the sword to his neck.

"You will relinquish Rhiannon if you would like to leave this place with your life," Pwyll yelled, more for the crowd than for Gwawl.

Gwawl's eyes were closed and he nodded quickly when Pwyll stated his terms. Pwyll sheathed his sword and raised his eyes to Rhiannon. She smiled at him emptily and felt her father patting his hand on her shoulder. As soon as Pwyll's eyes moved to the crowd, her smile dropped. The façade she was holding up was already starting to exhaust her and they weren't even married yet.

"Now you can forget about that silly little nymph," said Hefeydd Hên into her ear.

Rhiannon caught his eyes and she felt her own starting to widen. He held her gaze to confirm what he knew to have been the truth about her meetings with Alaw. His spies were peppered over the kingdom and it wouldn't have escaped his notice if his daughter had started an affair with a nymph. She made her way to Pwyll with her barren heart. Elated, the Prince grasped onto her cheeks and kissed her. Again, she made no movement to kiss him back.

Once Pwyll's father died, they would rule the kingdom of Dyfed as King and Queen. To the crowd, they may as well have been monarchs in those very moments. They roared in triumph and Rhiannon wondered whether she would be his wife by sunset. Her suspicions were proven to be right when her ladies led her back to the bed chambers. This time, they would prepare her for marriage.

~

Pwyll, above all else, desired an heir. Years passed in his marriage to Rhiannon and she had not yet sired an heir to the kingdom of Dyfed. His advisers were adamant that he left Rhiannon and took another wife to secure the future of the Crown. He took lovers that had likely sired him heirs, though they would all be illegitimate. He suspected that Rhiannon herself took lovers, but nothing resulted in a pregnancy. The people loved their new Queen but felt anxious that they would come to be with a child. Pwyll refused to marry another woman and insisted that Rhiannon would, in time, provide an heir to the throne.

Rhiannon would feel their prying eyes on her and her empty stomach. She was barren and quite certain of it. How could so much time have passed and she could not come to be with a child? Pwyll was relentless in his lovemaking and she never dared to refuse him. When he was away at night, she left for her own freedom. She fell into the arms of men and women alike but she never could quite forget Alaw. She saw her face and heard her voice in all the lovers that she found. Some would discuss her predicament and try to console her.

"I suppose they have not considered that he might be the one unable to provide me with a child," Rhiannon would say to them. "It is the fault in me, undoubtedly."

"Undoubtedly," her lovers would laugh.

In the third year of their marriage, Rhiannon felt the expected changes to her body. She was certain that she was carrying a child and she told Pwyll immediately. She didn't think anyone would concern themselves if it was Pwyll's if there was a child to finally take the throne. She prayed that the child would be a boy. Her father seemed convinced, from the strong kicks, that the child could be nothing but a boy. Rhiannon knew that, if it was a girl, she may well have to endure many more pregnancies to reach the boy who would take the throne.

To her relief, Rhiannon gave birth to a boy. To have said that her father and Pwyll were overjoyed would have been an understatement. There were feasts for days and parties that went long into the night. Meanwhile, Rhiannon lay in bed with the child and nursed him herself. The maids were sent in and they insisted on caring for the child as she rested during the night. Rhiannon could not help but wonder, after all the years, whether Alaw might have heard about the birth. She wondered whether the nymph was still alive. She wished, more than anything else, that she was there with her. Years could pass and she would love her no less than the day she laid eyes on her.

Pwyll allowed Rhiannon the time to bond with their son in her chambers. The maids would stay with her and take care of the child if he became too bothersome. They washed him and cooed at him day and night. Rhiannon wanted to leave the castle to go riding but felt bound to her room and the child that had become the reason for her existence. She would look from the small boy in his crib to the window of the tower. From this height, she could spot the woods where she met Alaw.

On a night like any other, Rhiannon and her maids fell asleep in her chambers. The boy slept in a small cot beside the window and caused little trouble in the night. Pwyll had ordered that a maid or Rhiannon herself should watch over the child every minute of every hour from day to night. The maid who was taking care of him that night fell fast asleep on her chair. Each maid was utterly exhausted from the work of constantly minding the young Prince.

A lone figure made his way to Rhiannon's tower. He escaped detection in the night and kept his dark hood over his head to conceal his identity. Reaching the tower, he sighed in wonder. How was it possible to have succeeded this far? He expected to die before reaching the door to Rhiannon's chambers. Instead, the Kingdom may as well have swung open the doors for this intruder.

Gwawl ap Clud opened the door as quietly as he could. He could not believe his luck when he saw that none of the maids were awake. He had weapons ready to silence them but found that he did not even need them. No blood would be spilled by his hands tonight as the heir to the throne was completely for the taking.

Gwawl took the sleeping boy in his arms and left the tower. He left as quietly as he had arrived and without a single person seeing how suspiciously he was acting.

Once he was completely out of earshot, Gwawl started to laugh. The child cried into the darkness of the night and Gwawl revelled in his triumph. He could only imagine the sorrow that Rhiannon and Pwyll would feel when they found their precious heir gone from his crib.

~

It was one of the maids who first found the cot empty. She suppressed the urge to scream and woke up the other maids in their chairs. Having taken a sleeping draught the night before, Rhiannon was sound asleep in her bed. The maid began to silently cry as she pointed at the empty cot and the maids began to search for the missing child in the room. One of the maids looked out of the window and only saw the usual sights of battlements and the lush green courtyard. There was no way that the baby was old enough to crawl. The other maids began to fear for their lives. They would all surely be killed for their incompetence by the King and Queen.

"What do we do? What do we do?" one of the maids whispered.

The other maid's mind was at work. She caught sight of Rhiannon's dog sleeping in his basket beside the bed and conjured up an idea that shocked them all. It was utter lunacy but, in their current states, they were ready to do anything to protect themselves.

"Kill the dog. We'll smear the blood over Rhiannon as she sleeps and make out that she devoured the child," said the maid.

"Will she not wake?" the other whispered.

"No," said the other maid. "I gave her a sleeping draught last night."

"Then let us make haste. It is our only hope to live another day."

The dog was killed and the crying maid smeared the blood over Rhiannon's hands, cheeks, and neck. They took the dog and the basket from the scene and made haste to execute their plan. Rhiannon continued to sleep through their deception and the maids readied themselves for the storm that would surely come.

Rhiannon awoke from her deep slumber and could not believe the sight that met her. Her blanket and bed sheets were smeared with blood, as well as her hands. She let out a shriek and the maids entered at once. She continued to scream and she ran to the cot immediately. Finding it empty, she let out a strangulated sob. Where was her boy and why was she covered in blood?

The maids went to find Pwyll at once and reported to him that they believed Rhiannon had devoured their son. Pwyll fell to his knees in anguish and disbelief. Had the pregnancy driven her completely mad? Pwyll raised his head to the three maids.

"That is impossible," he said to them. He ran to Rhiannon's chambers and found her screaming and writhing in the room.

"She has gone mad, my King," said the maid.

"Imprison her at once," said Pwyll.

Rhiannon was dragged from the chambers kicking and screaming. The guards locked her away in a cell and she screamed that a plot had been devised against her. She collapsed onto the floor and sobbed for the loss of her son as well as the loss of her own freedom. She clawed at the bars that prevented her from going out to find her son as she refused to believe that he was dead until she saw, with her own eyes, his body. She screamed Pwyll's name into the stone walls and begged for anyone to let her out.

~

News of Rhiannon's imprisonment reached the creatures of the forest in Dyfed. Having kept Rhiannon in her heart, Alaw grieved that she should be imprisoned. From what she had gathered, Alaw could not believe that her former lover could have ever devoured her own child. It sounded nothing like the Rhiannon she knew and loved.

Alaw lamented her fate and the fate of their relationship. She emerged from the river to the spot where they had spent many moons together. Her tears fell freely into the river and she found that they would not stop. She drowned the earth beneath her with her tears and felt her entire body beginning to turn to water. Alaw fell back into the river.

~

Eventually, Pwyll agreed to go to Rhiannon's cell. His steps were heavy as he descended into the darkness of the stone cells and his eyes were wet with tears when he saw his wife curled up on the floor. He could only accept now that his wife had descended into madness. To him, his wife was dead.

"Pwyll? Pwyll, is that you?"

Pwyll knelt behind Rhiannon's bars. "You would

consume your own child? Our child? The heir to the throne?"

"Pwyll, it is not true, I swear it," Rhiannon sobbed.

"How can I believe you? You were covered in blood," Pwyll snapped at her.

"It was a plot! I woke up and there was blood everywhere and our boy was gone," Rhiannon begged him to believe her.

"I will hear no more from you. I struggle to breathe the same air as you," Pwyll said before bringing himself back onto his feet and leaving Rhiannon in the darkness.

~

Gwawl left Rhiannon and Pwyll's child for the wolves. He left him in a blanket where they might find the boy and devour him for themselves. Gwawl did not waste another moment in the child's presence and left on his horse at once. Having exhausted himself from crying, the boy fell asleep in the blanket. By chance, no wolves passed through the path that day and the boy carried on sleeping in his blanket.

Teyrnon, Lord of Gwent-Is-Coed, walked through those woods to find his missing sheepdog. He searched far and wide to find his beloved sheepdog but his calling came to no avail. His sheepdog often went missing and he would find him drinking by a stream in the woods or lost on another farm. He checked every bit of the woods and even made sure to check the bushes where his dog might be resting. No stone went unturned as he searched those woods for his beloved dog.

Teyrnon did not expect to find a baby boy wrapped in a dirty blanket and fast asleep where the wolves might reach him. He picked up the child and started to try and find the boy's mother. He could see that there were wisps of gold hair peeking out of the top of his head and wondered whether his mother might have hair as gold as this. He found himself searching for the boy's parents as well as his sheepdog.

The sun was beginning to set and neither his sheepdog nor the boy's mother could be found. Teyrnon took the boy home with him and his wife couldn't believe her eyes. Over time, they gave up on trying to find the boy's mother and instead decided to take in the boy as their own son. Gwen, Teyrnon's wife, had not been able to conceive her own child and believed firmly that the boy had been sent from the heavens to them.

They called the boy Gwri Wallt Euryn for his gold hair. He grew up with the knowledge that he'd been found in the woods and that neither Teyrnon nor Gwen knew how he had come to be there. Gwri tried not to trouble himself with the details and comforted himself with the knowledge that Teyrnon and Gwen were his loving parents.

Meanwhile, something had started to trouble Teyrnon over the years. As the boy grew older and older, he saw a likeness in him that he had only seen in one man. Gwri Wallt Euryn bore such a likeness to the King of Dyfed that the resemblance was uncanny. As he grew into adolescence, the resemblance was unmistakable. Teyrnon did not voice his concerns to Gwen and instead hoped that his suspicions were wrong. He loved Gwri as his own son, yet he knew it would be a cruel injustice to keep his son from who may well be his true father. He had heard about the tale of Rhiannon's insanity and how she had purportedly devoured her own child. Could it have been that it was all a wicked lie and Gwri was the living proof?

On the eve of his sixteenth birthday, Teyrnon decided to take Gwri to Dyfed's court. The boy was ecstatic at the opportunity to go because he had lived his life working with his father on the farm. He was entranced by the riches of the court and the variety of people who walked in and out of those doors. Teyrnon watched his son come under the spell of Dyfed's court and he doubted that he could bring him back to the earth.

"Father! Father, look! Look! It's a painting of the King!" Gwri said enthusiastically.

"It is indeed," Teyrnon replied.

Teyrnon had informed the guards that there was an urgent matter to be addressed with the King. He showed them the boy and they tried to conceal their shock at his likeness to Pwyll. Far too many years had passed since the mysterious circumstances surrounding either his murder or disappearance and Rhiannon continued to fade away in prison. She was granted time to walk the grounds under strict supervision but her freedoms had been stripped away from her. The only shred of hope that kept her alive was that she had not seen, with her own eyes, that her son was dead. There was still the slither of hope that he might still live. Year after year, however, that hope continued to fade away.

It was explained to Pwyll that they believed his son was alive. He dropped all his responsibilities for the day and demanded that the boy be brought to him at once. The guards escorted Teyrnon and Gwri to the King, who himself rushed over to them as soon as they walked in through the huge wooden doors.

Pwyll put both hands onto Gwri's shoulders and inspected the boy. Gwri stared at the King and wondered whether he had done something wrong. In a matter of moments, Pwyll's eyes were swollen with tears and Teyrnon began to explain to the King the circumstances under which Gwri Wallt Euryn had been found as a boy.

Upon hearing the tale of his discovery, Pwyll felt a tremendous guilt set into his heart. He watched his son's eyes begin to widen with realisation and he felt his beginnings starting to piece back together. Gwri could not believe that his father was the King of Dyfed. He stared, open-mouthed, at the man adorned in Dyfed's riches.

"Get Rhiannon. Get Rhiannon at once," Pwyll said to the guards.

Rhiannon ran into the King's Hall as fast as her frail body would allow and the guards were hot on her tail. She ran, sobbing, towards where the boy who must have been her son, stood with Pwyll. She flung her arms around his slight body and heaved the grief of over a decade onto his young shoulders. Gwri held onto his mother's thin body and she would not stop repeating that she knew he was not dead. She swore that she would've felt his death had it happened. Such was the bond between the mother and child from the months she had carried him to the fateful night of his disappearance. A bond like that, she swore, could only be broken by death.

"Fy mhryder. My worry," she whispered to him.

Those were the first words she uttered to her son since he was stolen from her. From that moment onward, they knew Gwri Wallt Euryn as Pryderi, Prince of Dyfed, who was named after Rhiannon's agonising worry for him over the years.

The joy of being reunited with her son re-energised Rhiannon, yet the years of her imprisonment pressed heavily on her heart. Pwyll spent the rest of his days trying to regain Rhiannon's trust, but to little avail. Her marriage to Pwyll ended years ago when he refused to believe the truth of her innocence.

"What can I do to make amends?" Pwyll asked her after her release.

"Allow me my freedom again. Allow me to live an independent life," Rhiannon said.

Pwyll granted her request and Rhiannon came to live in her own home in a place she had not visited for many, many years near a river. After reuniting with her son, she took the long walk to the woods where she had truly felt free. The trees welcomed her back and the singing birds gathered to rejoice at her return. She could almost hear them chanting her name as they twittered above her head in the branches.

Rhiannon went to kneel by the river and she started to sing. She sang about her hiraeth, her longing for home and the home she had found in this place and in her lover. She sang and the singing birds joined her. When Rhiannon finished her song, she waited and hoped to hear the river's response.

"Rhiannon, is that you?" A voice asked from the depths of the river.

"Yes, Alaw," Rhiannon smiled. "Yes, it's me."

Branwen

The wind and rain battered down on them in Aberffraw that day. The sea was a torrent of vicious waves and the sands were whipped up in clouds across the shore. It wasn't surprising as they were out in the open waters and away from the safety of land on Anglesey. The marriage took place on the little church on an island surrounded by the waves and black rocks. There were only a few guests in attendance to witness the ceremony and one of them sat outside in the sea's waves. He rocked the waves, even as he sat idle on the seabed.

Bendigeid Frân, the giant, sat to wait for his sister and the King of Éire. A messenger was sent to inform him about the proceedings of the wedding in a boat. He plucked the boat from the sea with his fingertips and brought the tiny wooden vessel to his ear. The messenger relayed the events to his huge ear by shouting, though even then Bendigeid Frân strained his ears to listen over the roaring sound of the waves.

Branwen stared into the eyes of this foreign King and wondered why he had come to Cymru to disturb her peace. Perfectly content with her life, she lived in Harlech with her ladies as a free woman. Since the death of their parents, her brother Bendigeid Frân attended to her every need and looked after her like a father. She rode horses and went hunting like the men. Branwen was renowned for her beauty across the isles, but she prized her skills in hunting above all else.

Branwen stood in the church on the sea with a white veil over her face and a white dress on her body. She held a bouquet of flowers in her hands and stared at the Éireannach King in front of her. He came with his ships and army to seek her hand and an alliance with the Cymry. Their marriage would represent the unity between their lands and unite them across the sea that separated them. Bendigeid Frân had told his sister that he saw the ships from Harlech and knew instantly that it would be her hand that he sought. She barely had time to plea with her brother before she was made to prepare for the ceremony. Tears of salt stung her eyes after she cried for her future that was stolen so suddenly. Branwen did not know this man, nor did he know her. Had this marriage been arranged since their infancy? Did her late father fix it when she first emerged screaming from her mother's womb?

King Matholwch of Éire reached for Branwen's arms and held them when the priest asked them to repeat their vows. Meekly, Branwen repeated the Bible's words and listened to the stranger's voice repeat them with her. The Éireannach lords nodded their heads in approval, as did the lords of the Cymry. Branwen resisted the urge to sob and, after uttering the words, turned to her lady-in-waiting. She smiled at her and nodded for her to continue.

Branwen could see her brother outside of the church window, towering over them. She uttered the words that would seal the marriage in place and the King removed her veil. Matholwch bent to kiss her and she closed her eyes. His breath smelled like fish and salt. She resisted the urge to recoil before he pulled away. He held her hand and led her to the church door. Bendigeid Frân carried them back to the land on his palm and congratulated his sister on the marriage.

"How do you feel, sister?" Bendigeid Frân asked.

"Content," Branwen said, mindful that Matholwch stood directly beside her.

"You are now Queen of Éire," Bendigeid Frân said.

A feast was held in Aberffraw with music and entertainment for the evening. Branwen wanted the night to extend on and on as she had heard about all the things that would happen to her on her wedding night. Her ladies spoke about an unspeakable pain which would befall on them from God through her husband. She dreaded to think what this pain might be and insisted that the celebrations went far into the night. She might, with stalling, be able to delay this pain, perhaps even escape it.

In the corner of her eye, Branwen saw the doors of the hall swing open. A familiar figure passed through the hall in a fit of rage and she realised very quickly that it was her other brother, Efnisyen. Branwen stood and walked over to meet him. Efnisyen did not so much as look at her when he stormed over to Matholwch, who sat at the end of the long table. The laughter and chatter of the hall fell silent when Efnisyen approached the feast. He stood before the guests and clenched his fists.

"Why was I not informed about this?" he snapped. "My sister Branwen has been handed over for marriage and I was not given a second thought! The whole of Éire heard about this wedding before I did."

"Calm yourself, brother," Branwen begged. She held onto his arm but he did not take notice of her.

"You must be Efnisyen. A pleasure to meet you," Matholwch said. "I had not realised that you were ill-informed about the arrangements."

"No, I suppose you did not," Efnisyen sneered. "I must speak to Bendigeid Frân immediately."

Efnisyen left the hall and Branwen went to follow him, but Matholwch steered her back to her seat. The smell of salt no longer lingered around him; instead, she could smell the spirits on his breath. Her face twisted as the scent hit her senses. She felt her muscles seize as the heat of his hands seared into her bare flesh.

"Now, now, Branwen – do not fear. Your brother will be calm once more and he may join us to eat," Matholwch said.

Efnisyen climbed onto Bendigeid Frân's leg and waved his arms at him in rage. Bendigeid Frân implored his brother to be calm, but it only served to send him into an even stronger fit of anger.

"How dare you marry off our sister without my consent?" Efnisyen roared.

"You knew about the match, brother. I thought you had no issues with it," Bendigeid Frân said.

"I do not, but I would have appreciated a time and

place for the ceremony! I am her brother," Efnisyen said.

"You have been away!"

"And now I am here!" he snapped. "I have no use for your excuses, Bendigeid Frân. I must go and collect my wits."

Efnisyen clambered over Bendigeid Frân's trousered leg and stormed over to the stables. He made his way to find his horse to ride for the evening but found that the stables were filled with Éireannach horses. Efnisyen, in his fit of rage, took out his sword and slashed the necks of each Éireannach horse. They lay dead at his feet and he took the last living mare for himself. He rode away with the moonlight casting shadows over his path. The sounds from the hall quieted as he rode further away from the castle.

~

Branwen woke the next morning beside the Éireannach King. Her stomach was in knots and the bedsheets beneath her were spotted with blood. Her cheeks reddened with the thought of the King seeing the blood-stained sheets and she tried to conceal them with her body. Branwen only remembered the rocking, back and forth, like the ocean waves which surrounded the church yesterday morning. She could now speak about the pain the ladies had spoken about, once unspeakable.

At the time, she wondered if she would ever speak again. How could she have been so blind? She wanted Matholwch to leave so she might take the sheets to be washed. Branwen wanted to scrub herself clean from what had transpired between them. When he woke, he showered her with kisses and held her to him.

"I must leave you for the morning, my dear Branwen," Matholwch said. "Only to check the order of things with my men. I cannot escape my duties as King for long."

"Yes, of course," Branwen said. "You must go."

"Soon, we will sail to Éire. It will seem strange to leave home, but you will warm to my homeland in no time at all."

Branwen nodded, hoping that he would leave soon. She didn't think he had seen the sheets yet and so hoped they would escape his detection. Matholwch rose from the bed and Branwen watched him dress himself. She shivered from the cold morning air that swept through the window. As he buttoned up his shirt, she suddenly felt bare and so hugged the blanket over her body.

When he left, Branwen sprang from the bed and tore the bloodied sheets away and bundled them into a heap. Her lady-in-waiting found her sobbing at the bed and believing that the blood meant she would die. Branwen thanked God when the lady finally explained to her what it meant to have her hymen broken; she would live after all.

Matholwch made his way over to the hall and was immediately met by a crowd of Éireannach lords who were arguing amongst themselves. He ordered them to tell him, at once, what had caused so much uproar between them. They all argued about who would tell the King the news of the great insult that had been made known to them.

"We must take you to the stables, my King, to show you what has been done," said one of the lords.

Matholwch followed his lords to the stables and staggered back in shock to see the sight of the felled horses. They all lay coated in their own blood and utterly lifeless on the ground. Matholwch walked to the pen where his horse once stood. He knelt to touch the brown mane and vowed that he would do what he could to find the perpetrator.

The King and his men found Bendigeid Frân lying asleep by the castle. It took a crowd of them to yell into his ear to awaken the giant. When he heard the news from Matholwch, he was distraught.

"I do not know who dared to insult you in this way, Matholwch, but I can assure you that everything will be done to discover the culprit," Bendigeid Frân said.

"I thank you, Bendigeid Frân, for your kindness. However, I must admit that this has been a blow to my men and I," Matholwch admitted.

"Indeed, it has," Bendigeid Frân said. "To apologise for this insult, your men will receive new horses. In addition, I will give you a cauldron with great power."

"A cauldron?"

"Yes. The cauldron is one that can restore the dead back to life," said the giant.

Matholwch and his men raised their eyebrows to one another. Bendigeid Frân ordered that the cauldron be retrieved from the castle dungeons and given as a gift to Matholwch and the Éireannach lords. King Matholwch inspected the cauldron and felt the magic pulsating into his fingers as he touched its rim. The lords thanked Bendigeid Frân endlessly and promised to treasure the cauldron in Éire for years and years to come. Matholwch bowed to the giant and thanked him for the great gift.

"In exchange, I hope that my sister Branwen will be cared for well in your lands."

"I give you my word, Bendigeid Frân," Matholwch said.

The ships were prepared for their departure and Branwen could hardly be consoled when she realised how soon they would leave for Éire. Bendigeid Frân assured her that she would be able to take her lady-in-waiting and that her every need would be met. He also assured her that he would meet her again, even if it meant he had to cross the Éireannach sea to see her.

Branwen stood in her brother's palm and rested her head on his thumb. She embraced the place between his finger and thumb and allowed her tears to fall onto his skin. Branwen made her way down again to her husband and farewelled her brother. Efnisyen was nowhere to be seen.

Branwen waved at Bendigeid Frân as the ships moved away from the land. She watched the land disappear into the horizon for hours and she could only make out the outline of Bendigeid Frân's body. Matholwch tried to comfort her in her grief but found her unresponsive. She felt that she had been severed from her homeland and yearned to return soon. Her hiraeth was beginning to plague her already and she had barely left Cymru's shores. Branwen did not know Éire and she feared that she would not be at home there in the way that she felt at home in Cymru.

Matholwch led Branwen to the other side of the ship. He turned her around and away from Cymru. He pointed in the distance towards Éire and Branwen could make out the faint outlines of land. At the sight of the land, she suddenly felt renewed at the prospect of arriving there. She asked Matholwch if women hunted in Éire and he assured her that she would be granted the liberty.

Branwen felt like kissing the land when they arrived in Éire. Sea sickness plagued her for the entire duration of the journey and she hoped not to have to travel on the sea for a long while. Matholwch took her to his castle, which would be her new home, and reassured her that she would be made comfortable.

~

Over time, Branwen came to love the land. She missed her family and Cymru dearly but found a thrill in discovering this new place. She found that the cure to her hiraeth for home simply lay in discovering the secrets of this new one.

Matholwch summoned her to the hall and she could not guess why she would be summoned so formally by her husband. She made her way through the lavish corridors in a new dress that had been handmade for her on arrival. Branwen skipped into the hall with a smile on her face and she even felt, now, that she could love this King.

"Branwen," he said. "I have some very grave news indeed."

Branwen watched the joy in his face quickly fading away and he pulled away from her touch. She felt a pain greater than what she had experienced with him on their wedding night and tears began to quickly fill her eyes.

"What is wrong, Matholwch?" she asked.

"We have been tricked by your brother Bendigeid Frân. The cauldron he gave to us does indeed bring the dead back to life, but the cauldron's power also strikes them deaf and blind," Matholwch said.

"Husband, you must know I knew nothing of this –" Branwen started.

"Your brothers are not here to receive the punishment for this insult. You, on the other hand, are here," Matholwch said.

"What? What do you mean?" Branwen cried. "The cauldron still works, doesn't it?"

Matholwch lowered his head and his eyes dropped to the stone floor. Branwen felt hands on her arms which led her away from her husband. She cried out to him and begged that her brothers might be forgiven.

"Am I not your wife, Matholwch?" Branwen yelled from the doorway as Matholwch's men led her away. "How could you do this to me?"

"Tá brón orm, Branwen," Matholwch said. "Sadness is upon me now."

As punishment for her brother's deception, Branwen found herself banished to the kitchens to work. Every day, she worked with the other kitchen staff to endure her punishment. She prepared meals and feasts for the

King and felt the sting of her cruel treatment for an insult she had not committed. Branwen prayed, day and night, that she might be rescued by her brothers in Cymru. Her contact with the outside world was severed and she had no means to inform them about what had happened. For all she knew, her husband might be the one to send letters over the sea to tell her brothers that she was well.

Branwen only saw Matholwch in the night. She slept in her unfurnished chamber and dreaded the moment when she would hear her door creak open. In the darkness, he would slither in like a burglar and undress himself beside her bed. Branwen felt her body become hot with fear and her eyes stung from her crying.

Matholwch's body smelled like sweat and alcohol. He would join her in the bed and pin her down. Night after night, he raped her and then immediately left her rooms. Sometimes, he stayed until morning and she would see what had become of him. His face had aged and hardened since she last saw him in the daylight.

Branwen missed the mountains of Cymru and the beach in Harlech. When grieving for her former life, she would recall the golden coasts and the craggy mountains of her home. She would take herself back to a time when she could hunt freely and roam the fields of her homeland. Branwen wondered, in her hiraeth, if she would ever see them again.

In the space of months, Branwen noticed a change in her body. She pressed her palms against her naked stomach and found herself vomiting in the bowls left beside her bed. When working in the kitchens, Branwen carried the weight of her own body around and felt constantly like she could collapse in a heap onto the floor. It was only Matholwch who, when visiting her at night, noticed that she was carrying his child. The next morning, he ordered that Branwen was moved from the servants' quarters.

"She must be made comfortable. She carries the heir to the throne," Matholwch said. "Take her to a more suitable room and give her a lady to attend to her needs."

Branwen's pregnancy proved to be a difficult one. She carried the child in her stomach and felt the bundle of flesh protest the cage of her body. Matholwch hoped with every passing day that the child would be a boy to inherit the throne and Branwen hoped for nothing more than to be rid of the pain.

The childbirth was difficult and Branwen screamed well into dawn as the birds rose. The crows were no match for her screaming and Matholwch swore that everyone in Éire could hear her. The baby joined her screaming and she reached her arms out for the child in relief. The servants took the child away from Branwen's arms and Matholwch demanded to know whether it was a boy. He rejoiced until he remembered that the boy had to be named by his mother.

"She must name him, as is customary," Matholwch said, unable to meet her eye.

"Gwern," Branwen said. "I will call him Gwern."

"Very well. Let us go." Matholwch said to the servants.

"Where are you going? Where are you taking him? He must be with his mother –" Branwen yelled.

Matholwch and the servants took the child away and Branwen screamed at them. The screams that came from her were unlike any sound she had made during Gwern's birth. The ladies held her back onto the bed until she passed out in exhaustion.

~

Bendigeid Frân thought about his sister Branwen every day. He received word from Matholwch and even a few notes from Branwen herself over the sea that separated them. He grieved the loss of his sister but felt content that she enjoyed her life in Éire so much. He was eager to see his nephew Gwern and hoped to hear word that they might see one another again. The two years they had spent apart stretched like centuries between them.

Bendigeid Frân would often sit near the hills above Harlech and Porthmadog in Gwynedd. He would look out over the sea and wonder whether Branwen gazed in the same direction. From here, he would receive messages from the birds that flew from Éire with the letters tied to their little legs. He could see, in the distance, a small bird that he could not quite make out. He brought a magnifying glass, one that rested atop the hill, to his eye so that he could see the bird. A lone starling carried a note on its leg above the sea waves and looked ready to collapse in exhaustion.

The starling arrived and rested on Bendigeid Frân's hand. He beckoned one of his men to read the letter out to him. He knew it must be a letter from Branwen. When one of the men read it out, Bendigeid Frân's eyes watered and made rivers that led out to the sea. His men ran away from the deluge and Bendigeid Frân lifted the man who stood at his ear to read out the rest of Branwen's letter. It had taken Branwen two years to tame the starling that brought the letter and two years for him to discover how cruelly she had been treated. Branwen, through the kitchen window, tamed the bird to send the letter across the Éireannach sea.

"I want our armies to be readied for war. Matholwch will not get away with this," Bendigeid Frân said.

Efnisyen, who himself yearned to fight, gathered the armies that would cross the Éireannach sea. Bendigeid Frân, being his enormous size, would carry himself across the ocean waters. He waded through the sea with the ships beside him and waved away the clouds from his eyes. Bendigeid Frân saw the shores of Éire before anyone else and felt the sudden urge to sprint across the sea. His feet could easily break the ocean surface and send waves to deluge their land. Then, he would trample across their fields, castles, and churches. He could devastate their land in a matter of moments. The only thing which stopped him was the risk of killing his sister and the nephew he had not yet met.

On land, Matholwch received word from his messengers about the incoming fleet. They told him that the Cymry would soon arrive on their shores. Enraged, he made his way down to the kitchens of his castle to find his wife. Matholwch swung open the wooden door and stood on the threshold. The door flew off the hinges and Branwen felt her spirit leave her body. She turned to find her husband clenching his fists with a flame-red face and a frown knitted on his brow. Holding onto the counter-top, she stepped away from where he stood.

Matholwch glared at Branwen from the threshold. He took slow steps from the doorway towards her. Branwen cursed herself for not having a knife on the counter-top beside her. In those moments, she didn't doubt that Matholwch would kill her. He had his heir and she was utterly useless to him now. She heard the servants yelling in a flurry of emotion and they exclaimed that the Cymry were here to attack them. Branwen felt her heart soar that her message from the tamed starling had reached her brothers. Now, her heart sank; she may not live to see them after all.

Matholwch grabbed onto Branwen's arms and

brought her face close to his. He dipped his mouth to her ear and Branwen felt a sob begin to form at the pit of her stomach. It was this force that she feared every night before he raped her in the darkness. She tried writhing out of his grasp, but his grip was far too firm for her to move an inch. She scrunched up her eyes when she felt his hot breath against her ear.

"You sent for them, didn't you?" he whispered. "Tell me."

"I did not," Branwen lied. "I did no such thing –"

"Lies. How did you do it? Are you a witch, Branwen? Did you charm one of my messengers?" Matholwch asked.

"No, I did not. I beg you to let me go," Branwen said.

"But how did they find out, Branwen? Do you truly believe that I am as much of a fool as that?" he replied.

Matholwch let Branwen go and she breathed again. Before she caught herbreath, he lifted his hand and struck her across the face. Branwen staggered and reached out both hands to catch the blow. She fell onto the stone floor in a huge thud and the pain travelled deep into her body. She felt herself becoming hotter and her eyes burned with tears.

Matholwch left the kitchen and made haste to find his messengers. He gathered the Éireannach lords and informed them that they must begin to prepare for war. The lords, having enjoyed this period of peace, were not pleased to hear this news.

"Have you destroyed all the bridges from the sea?" Matholwch asked one of his generals.

"No, my King, we await your orders –"

"Do so at once!" he snapped. "There are rivers that those men cannot cross without a bridge. It gives us time to gather our forces."

~

The Cymry arrived on the land to find those same bridges had been destroyed. They turned to Bendigeid Frân and Efnisyen for orders on what to do next. Bendigeid Frân could see, from his great height, how the Éireannach men had laid waste to their own bridges to keep them out. He let out a laugh and knelt on the riverbed.

Bendigeid Frân placed both hands on either side of where the bridge once stood and lay his body between them. Efnisyen laughed in triumph and told his men to use Bendigeid Frân as their bridge to the land. One by one, the men walked with their weapons across Bendigeid Frân's body. Efnisyen patted his brother's stomach as he went across and laughed that the Éireannach had been duped.

When news of this came to Matholwch, he fell into a fit of rage. He became terrified that he would walk into a war that he had no means of winning. Desperate, he returned to the kitchens where Branwen worked. Her face was bruised purple from Matholwch's violence and she refused to speak a word to anyone. When she saw Matholwch enter, she reached for the knife beside her and held it up to him. Matholwch stepped back and held out his hands.

"I want to end this war, Branwen. Tell me how I can do it," Matholwch begged. "I am not here to harm you."

Branwen held the knife firmly in her palm and narrowed her eyes at him. She could not tell whether he was truly desperate. Sensing this hesitation, Matholwch knelt on his two knees before her and buried his face in his hands. Branwen lowered the knife towards where he knelt and frowned at him.

"To end it, you must show them a kindness, especially Bendigeid Frân," Branwen said.

"What kindness? I will do anything," Matholwch said.

"Make him a house and hut in his honour. You must also guarantee mine and Gwern's safety, otherwise he will not listen," Branwen said.

Matholwch rose from his knees, knowing what he needed to do. He left Branwen for a second time and ordered that his messengers come to him at once. Bendigeid Frân and Efnisyen awaited word from him as they crossed even more rivers in Éire to reach the castle. A flustered messenger reached them and relayed the details of Matholwch's letter.

"King Matholwch has assured Branwen and Gwern's safety. He intends to offer you a boon and he has promised that Gwern will inherit the Éireannach throne. He does not want war," the messenger said quickly.

"Very well – we will hold off. I will await his word on this boon he mentions. As for Branwen and Gwern, I cannot trust his word. Efnisyen, I believe you should investigate this," Bendigeid Frân said.

"With pleasure, brother." Efnisyen replied.

In disguise, Efnisyen crossed miles and miles of land in Éire to reach Matholwch's castle. He enjoyed the anonymity that his disguise offered and how easily he could move from one place to the other. He questioned people in taverns, on walkways and near farms. He discovered, through bribery, where his nephew Gwern was being nursed. He made his way to the cottage where the maids nursed him. He dressed as a doctor and acted the part for the maids at the door.

"I insist that I must see the baby to check on his health. The King has ordered it," Efnisyen said.

"Of course, doctor. Please come in," one of the maids said.

Efnisyen walked through the cluttered cottage and insisted that he was left to his work. The maids refused to leave him alone with the boy and this angered Efnisyen. He brandished a knife and immediately went about murdering the two maids. Gwern started to cry when he heard their screams tearing through the air of the cottage. Lifeless, the maids lay in a pool of their own blood on the wooden floorboards.

Efnisyen took the child in his arms and sat in the old maid's armchair near the hearth. He managed to silence Gwern by wrapping him in a warm blanket and rocking him in his arms. He cooed at his nephew and spent an hour sitting with him by the fire.

This was the longest Gwern had spent with someone who shared his blood. He gazed down at Gwern and realised that he had deprived the child of the wet nurse that lay in her own blood at his feet. Efnisyen's mind went to work with thoughts about what part this small child had to play in this war.

"I must deprive Matholwch of his son and an heir to the throne," Efnisyen whispered to Gwern. "Even if it means that I must deprive my sister of a son too."

Efnisyen stood from the armchair with Gwern in his arms. The flames from the fire licked the air and the firewood crackled with sparks. Parts of the fire turned grey with ash and disintegrated into flakes. Efnisyen unwrapped the child from the blanket and held him in his two hands. He brought the baby towards the flames and let them devour him. He dropped him into the fire and watched his flesh burn.

~

Efnisyen left the cottage with blood crusting between the fingers on his hands. He continued to walk amongst the Éireannach in his disguise and delayed his return to the Cymry. Efnisyen knew that Bendigeid Frân would not let him live once he discovered what he had done. It would break Branwen's heart, but he sought only to break Matholwch's and cause chaos amongst the Éireannach. He thirsted for war and knew that this would be the spark to cause it. He craved bloodshed and yearned to decimate the Éireannach army.

When word reached Matholwch about Gwern, he was lost in his rage. He could only assume that one of the Cymry had done it and he demanded to know exactly who had murdered his son. He despaired that his son, the heir to the throne, was lost to them and the Éireannach lords knew that war was becoming more and more imminent.

"What will be our next steps, my King?" one of the Éireannach lords asked.

"We will use the cauldron against them in battle," Matholwch said. "In whatever way we can."

The news reached Branwen about Gwern's murder and she felt her chest tighten. Her heart sank and she could not stop the wave of sobs which overcame her. She knelt to the floor in the kitchens and wailed that it could not be true. In her frenzy, she couldn't understand how this could happen. She tried to tear out her hair but the maids held her arms and tried to calm her.

"It cannot be. They would not kill him. He is my son. Who, out of the Cymry, would do this? Bendigeid Frân would never have ordered his death. Gwern is his nephew."

Branwen writhed on the ground and continued to scream well into the night. She refused to believe them and demanded to see Gwern at once. The servants spoke about declarations of war but Branwen could not have cared less. War could rage outside of her rooms and she would only think about the loss of her son. She, like Matholwch, felt determined to discover who could have ordered and committed such a crime.

The Éireannach and the Cymry met on the battlefield with their horses and weapons. They battled and the Éireannach soldiers who fell were immediately thrown into the cauldron. Once revived, they returned to the battlefield. They dipped their weapons into the cauldron to enchant them and they steeled themselves against the attack. The Cymry watched this unfold and knew that their only chance was to use Bendigeid Frân against them.

Efnisyen, who had not returned to the Cymry, stood disguised as an Éireannach soldier. He stood among the ranks of the enemy's army with a plan to execute. He went to lay amongst the dead soldiers who were being hauled into the cauldron and acted as though he himself were one of the dead. An Éireannach soldier threw the bodies into the cauldron and watched them emerge alive. He lifted Efnisyen's body from the ground and threw him into the cauldron. Efnisyen felt its liquid power envelop his body and he began to push his arms and legs against the cauldron's walls.

The cauldron burst and its walls shattered like glass. Efnisyen's body spilled out, dead, and the Éireannach men despaired at the loss of the cauldron. The man who informed Matholwch was killed on the spot for the news and the Éireannach were suddenly powerless without their weapon against the Cymry.

Bendigeid Frân saw the cauldron in pieces in the distance and knew that the flow of Éireannach soldiers would cease after its destruction. He could not understand why the cauldron had been destroyed and did not know that his own brother lay among the dead. He heard of Gwern's murder and could only guess that his brother Efnisyen had committed the crime. He despaired that the news would reach Branwen and felt responsible for having sent Efnisyen to the boy.

The cauldron is lost, Matholwch thought. The messenger lay dead at the feet of his horse and he despaired that they would lose the war. He knew that their chances were slim against the giant Bendigeid Frân, but the cauldron's power shielded them. Desperate, Matholwch dipped his arrowhead into a vial of poison and aimed it directly at Bendigeid Frân. Bendigeid Frân saw Matholwch among the men and felt a rage grip him. The giant intended to destroy the King's armies and find Branwen but he quickly realised that she was not amongst them.

~

Branwen rode on a horse towards the place where the battle commenced. She remembered the days when she went hunting or accompanied her brother Efnisyen through the woods. She remembered the freedom she felt in those moments and how she could have spent the rest of her days perfectly content in this way. Now, she felt her heart contracting and her freedom withering into nothingness.

Branwen reached the battlefield and found the Éireannach ranks in utter chaos. She saw her brother, Bendigeid Frân, laying waste to the Éireannach men and she caught sight of her husband, Matholwch, aiming at him. Branwen screamed at him to lower his weapon but he had already loosed the arrow.

Matholwch shot the poisoned arrow and it struck Bendigeid Frân in his eye. He roared in pain and staggered back. The earth rumbled and he fell onto his back. The land behind him lifted from the impact and sent waves of dirt across the Éireannach fields. Matholwch yelled out in victory and his men rejoiced that the giant had fallen.

Branwen rode her horse through the fallen soldiers to reach her brother. Bodies lay strewn across the ground and their blood stained the earth alongside the arrows and swords that lay scattered across the ground. Matholwch rejoiced until he saw the lone horse riding through the carnage. Matholwch realised that the black-haired rider was his wife. He remembered their son and a numbness seeped into his body. Branwen reached the Cymry and they lowered their weapons when they realised that it was a woman who approached them and none other than Branwen herself. She dismounted near Bendigeid Frân's ear and placed her hands on his face.

"My brother – I am here. It is me, your sister, Branwen," she said to him.

The poisoned arrow sent waves of unimaginable agony through his eye but he softened when he strained to hear his sister's voice. He knew that the poison on the arrow would kill him and there was nobody else in the world he would rather have spent his last moments with.

"How can I ever make amends for what I did? I sent you to this Éireannach King and you have suffered under him for years," Bendigeid Frân said.

"There is nothing to forgive," Branwen said. "He treated me ill and it is no fault of yours. But brother, you must tell me who killed Gwern."

Bendigeid Frân despaired. He did not think he could bear to tell his sister about the grave mistake he had made in trusting their brother. He knew of Efnisyen's faults and was foolish enough to have trusted him to find Gwern. Instead, he had disappeared and Gwern had been found dead in the fireplace of a cottage.

"I sent our brother, Efnisyen, to discover Gwern's whereabouts and reassure me of his and your safety," Bendigeid Frân said. "I did not send him to kill Gwern. I swear it, sister."

Branwen's heart fell in her chest. She could hardly believe that Efnisyen, her own brother, could have murdered her son, who was also his nephew. She placed her hand on her heart and lowered her head. With her other hand, Branwen comforted Bendigeid Frân. He felt her small hand caressing his cheek and he felt a great fatigue overcome him.

"Fy mrawd. My brother – do not leave me," Branwen whispered against him.

"Fy chwaer... I am here," Bendigeid Frân said. "My sister, Branwen."

The poison took Bendigeid Frân's life and his body became a part of the hill in Éire. Branwen lay beside him and refused to move away. When the armies retreated, they remained beside one another. She felt the loss of her family hanging heavy on her young shoulders and wished only, in her grief, to join them.

"Gwae fi o'm genedigaeth," Branwen said. "Woe it is that I was ever born."

Branwen remained kneeling on the earth beside Bendigeid Frân and placed her forehead on the dirt beside him as if in prayer. Matholwch left his men to find her still kneeling beside the giant. He placed his hand on her shoulder and felt that it was limp beneath his fingers. The heat of her body had already begun to leave and there she remained, lifeless beside her brother.

The Cymry insisted on taking Branwen's body back to her homeland with Bendigeid Frân's head. They severed the head from his body and carried it on a ship towards home. Branwen was laid to rest on a pyre of wood and carried on the same ship home. Both brother and sister were burnt beside the Afon Alaw and their ashes were scattered. Their dust danced in the water, free, until they rejoined the sea.

Arianrhod

"King Math – here I present to you the fairest, most beautiful woman to walk this land – Arianrhod, daughter of Dôn," Gwydion said.

Arianrhod stepped forward, gleaming, and bowed to Math, King of Gwynedd. She kept her eyes trained to the floor until he bade her to rise. Her head swam from the red carpet beneath her feet. She listened to them talking and felt her back straining from her exaggerated bow.

This was no average ceremony. The women who stood in line behind her claimed they were the fairest and most beautiful in all of Cymru. Courtiers and guests mingled with royalty and the hall bustled with people who were laughing and drinking. Up until the ceremony, King Math snapped at the waiting staff who tripped over their own feet to bring him refreshments and any smatterings of gossip that circulated the hall.

Goewin, the King's former footholder, sat in the corner of the room in shame. Her body shook whenever she heard the King yell at his waiting staff. Her head drooped and she let the hot tears flow down her face. Only virgins could act as the King's footholder and she was now stripped of the position.

Goewin wrung her dress between her hands and blew her nose on her sodden handkerchief. Nobody stood there to comfort her and so she let out a torrent of emotions for all to see. When one of her sobs became audible to the guests, the King ordered that a maid take her away from the hall at once.

Arianrhod glanced at Goewin's sagging body and wondered what future lay ahead for her. The King needed a new footholder as Goewin had been raped by one of his horsemen. She would surely be forced to marry the man and even find herself banished from the court. Arianrhod's stomach clenched with the thought. She would have done anything to avoid such a fate. It would have brought shame on her and severed the alliance her family had with the court. They enjoyed the riches of the King's castle and Arianrhod could imagine living out her days here. It was the reason why she chose to stand in line with the other women.

All the women who preceded Arianrhod were taken away. One was dragged away crying and screaming as the King surveyed the next in line. Arianrhod, being the last, tried to distract herself from the sounds of crying and the King's admonishments.

"Not thin enough."

"She isn't pleasing to look at."

"Not dainty in the slightest."

Each admonishment sent a blow to the women and Arianrhod tried not to fear. She surveyed the hall in all its glory and thought about how being a footholder in this grand castle would secure her future. She looked up at the jewelled seats and imagined herself at the King of Gwynedd's feet with enough riches to last a lifetime. Gowns would be made ready for her, and food would never be scarce.

The women who preceded Arianrhod walked away, disgraced, with their hearts heavy from a single sweep of Math's hand. Arianrhod took a brief look over to her brother Gwydion, the King's magician, for reassurance. Her brother stood on the King's right-hand side and had so far made the announcements for each woman's birth and their credentials. Arianrhod smiled at Gwydion and he winked at her discreetly. She would be the next footholder, and with her brother's help she would secure the position for the rest of her days. And now, here she was, bowing before the King. It was her turn to glow.

"Yes, she is beautiful indeed, and fair. A gem to your family name, Gwydion. You have been a loyal magician, and your sister would be a loyal footholder to me," King Math of Gwynedd said. "However, I cannot simply accept her as such. To be my footholder, she must be pure of heart and body. Have you, fair lady, been pure?"

"Yes, my King," Arianrhod said.

"Gwydion, take out the rod," King Math said. "And rise, fair lady, so that I may see you in the light."

Arianrhod rose from her bow and the King nodded in approval. Gwydion waved his fingertips in the air and a silver rod appeared on the floor before her, glimmering beneath the candlelight. Gwydion enchanted it and Arianrhod watched the rod slither along the carpet.

"Step over the rod. It will test your purity," said the King.

Arianrhod stood tall with all the eyes of the hall on her. She inhaled deeply and lifted her foot. Her family, friends, loyal maidens and guests watched in anticipation as she started to step foot across the silver rod. One foot landed on the other side and she exhaled. Arianrhod, determined now to pass the test, brought her other foot to join it.

For a split second, she thought she'd succeeded. She readied herself to turn around and smile at her brother and the King. But, like an ocean wave crashing over her, she felt her body flood with sweat. A stabbing pain shot through her stomach and she squeezed her eyes shut.

Two slithering creatures poured onto the carpet and Arianrhod fell, reeling with shock. The hall gasped as the two beings emerged from the folds of her white dress. They slithered down her thighs and onto the floor in two balls of flesh. One was blue, resembling a sea monster, and the other looked like a human baby enveloped in a transparent ball. The guests stepped away, widening the circle around Arianrhod. The King recoiled in disgust when he saw the creatures pooling on the floor.

Arianrhod screamed in horror. All the other sounds of the hall were drowned by the gut-wrenching scream that tore through her body. She lifted her head blearily, catching sight of the blue beast crawling across the floor. How had something so beast-like emerged from her body? Arianrhod later heard it had been thrown into the sea and lived as a spirit of the waters. She stared at the human baby that lay in a heap of fluid on the floor. It didn't move nor make a sound, likely dead at birth.

Arianrhod looked up at Gwydion. He gazed down at her in disgust and refused to even hold out a hand to help her. Rage gripped her and she pointed her finger at him.

"This is your fault! You did this," she yelled for all the hall to hear. "My own brother."

Gwydion turned his head and beckoned the servants. Arianrhod screamed again and she was dragged away by multiple hands. Grief welled inside her for all that had occurred in those brief few moments. She watched the hall vanish from her eyes, all the candlelight, laughter and joy. She sobbed and sobbed, unable to stop the flood of tears from escaping her. Shame bubbled inside her gut and she felt the numbness set in.

Gwydion watched as his sister was pulled away. The entire hall was in uproar and the human baby on the floor was forgotten, something discarded carelessly on the ground. The King waved his hands at some of his servants and ordered them to find more virgins immediately. He would surely take any who could step over the rod.

Gwydion approached the baby on the floor and realised quickly that it was a boy. Gwydion lifted him, oozing with liquid, and felt his blood pumping, alive, on his fingertips. He took the baby boy away from the hall and carried him to his private rooms. Gwydion set him down on a table and plied open the folds of liquid that enveloped him. In one burst, when the air reached him, the boy started to cry.

Gwydion opened a chest in his room and enchanted it to let the boy rest inside. Once Arianrhod was banished, he would raise the boy in the court and find a use for him.

~

Arianrhod, banished from the King of Gwynedd's court, came to live on a remote fortress on the sea. The fortress, surrounded by black rocks, was west of Llandwrog and far enough away from the court. It was now called Caer Arianrhod. She lived with a couple of maids on the caer and Gwydion enchanted it to prevent her from leaving the desolate island.

Despairing for her future, Arianrhod felt that she would wither away on this remote place and die. She'd considered hauling herself out of the castle and onto the rocks for a swift end but felt the need for revenge burning. She would live to one day slight the King and her so-called brother. If she lived, there was hope.

A few months after she'd been banished from the court, Gwydion sent his sister a visitor. Arianrhod watched from the caer as a familiar figure came out of the boat and walked between her two maids. She saw the familiar brown braids hanging down to her waist and her careful walk up to the entryway. Arianrhod ran to the door and opened it, welcoming in the guest with open arms. The visitor who came on the boat was none other than Goewin.

"Why did Gwydion send you here?" Arianrhod asked.

"Gwydion didn't send me - I wanted to come here," Goewin said. "I asked him if I could come and he relented."

Arianrhod, feeling a certain kinship with this fallen woman, welcomed her in and they cried together as the sea wind hammered against the fortress walls. They embraced and confided in one another about their exile. Fearing for her life, Goewin asked to stay with Arianrhod in her fortress. The man who raped her was married to another woman and therefore Goewin was destitute. She was allowed to stay and Arianrhod felt hope kindle in their newfound friendship.

The sky burned red from the sun that set over them that night. They vowed to always protect and support one another, no matter what challenges came to face them. The sea battered against the rocks and the wind roared through the caer's windows. They promised that they would weather the storm together and find happiness in their exile.

Goewin spent her days knitting until her fingers reddened and Arianrhod read book after book until her eyes burned. At the end of each day, the women watched the waves outside of the caer and pointed at the boats and seagulls. Arianrhod hoped that her son, the sea creature, was faring well in these waters. She thought about him each time she looked out onto the waves.

They knew the sea by now and the way it danced, and even raged. When the waters were still and the wind quiet, they would venture out onto the rocks and skim stones that rippled the surface. They laughed and sang with the maids, capturing what glimmers of joy they could in their exile. When they argued, they brought the sea to shame with their roaring, until they forgave one another and brought peace to the caer.

Over time, Goewin and Arianrhod came to be lovers. They met each morning and closed each day together. Their friendship blossomed into a deep love for one another. The love they shared grew with every passing day and they yearned to spend every waking moment in each other's presence. Arianrhod and Goewin lived and breathed for each other and felt that it was only natural to share a room and sleep together.

The women made the caer their home. Goewin and the maids would bring supplies from the village of Llandwrog once a week and the odd book or trinket. A man on a boat would arrive, every Friday, to take them to the land to restock. Arianrhod, from Gwydion's curse, forgot what the land felt like, what the trees were and how they changed. She remembered the land from how the women spoke about it.

Arianrhod could see the coast of Dinas Dinlle in the distance and, every so often, she could make out figures on the beach. She forgot what different faces looked like. She grew so accustomed to Goewin, the maids and the boat man that she believed they were the only people left on the face of the earth. Arianrhod knew the ocean waves and the roar of the wind better than she knew the people that walked on the land.

~

Gwydion, without Arianrhod's knowledge, raised the son she had birthed in the court. He grew over the years and dove headlong into boyhood. Gwydion took his nephew under his wing and taught him most of what he knew, besides his precious magical abilities. The boy was skilled at crafting, building and especially accurate when he threw stones at targets. His eye was sharper than any that Gwydion had ever known.

"Well done, young boy. You are improving every day," Gwydion said on the eve of his eighth birthday. "It is about time that you were given a name, but it cannot be from me."

"Who, uncle, will give me a name?" The boy asked.

"Your mother, Arianrhod. You will meet her and she will name you."

"Can you not name me, uncle? Must it be my mother?"

"No, my boy, I cannot name you," Gwydion replied. "It is tradition that the first words uttered to you by your mother shall be your name."

Arianrhod received word from her brother that, after eight years on the caer, she would be granted her freedom from exile. She felt a lightness in her step after Gwydion lifted the enchantment and felt a yearning to see and feel the land again. For years, she had been a part of the sea, but she was no sea creature. She yearned to feel the earth beneath her feet again and touch the barks of the trees. She missed her family dearly, but she knew there was no way of returning to them again, even after so much time.

On the day of her release, Arianrhod prepared to leave the caer. Goewin helped her onto the old boat and the boat man rowed them to the shore. Arianrhod watched the land coming closer and closer to her, as though it came to meet her on arrival. Goewin held her hand and kissed her forehead.

"Paid a bod ofn, Arianrhod. Don't be afraid. The land welcomes you home," Goewin said.

Arianrhod closed her eyes and felt the sea wind caress her face. The wind whispered in her ear and she felt the land draw nearer. When the boat reached the shore, Goewin helped Arianrhod onto the soft sand. She collapsed to her knees and buried her face to the ground. She gathered sand in her hands and balled them into fists. Goewin knelt beside her and, after a time, led her towards the dunes. The grass of the dunes swayed in the distance with the force of the wind, as though they beckoned her onward. Arianrhod walked through the fine sand and relished in the feel of the speckles that stuck between her fingers. She ran her fingers through the dune grass and walked out of the sand. The earth hardened beneath her feet and she knelt to touch the ground.

Arianrhod's face, wet with tears, broke into a smile. She took away her boots and felt the grass kiss the soles of her feet. Arianrhod ran, laughing, and Goewin struggled to catch up with her. Her dress flew around her in the wind and she waved her arms at Goewin from a distance. Arianrhod, in those brief moments, fell in love with the land again.

A week after her release, Gwydion sent word to his sister about a meeting. He had arranged for her, Goewin and the maids to live in a small house in the woods, not far from Llandwrog. Arianrhod agreed, reluctantly, to meet with her brother. She sent him two words, by hand, for him to read in advance: "No tricks." She knew she needed to be on her guard. Her brother, versed in the magical arts, could deceive her with a simple wave of his hand.

Gwydion knocked the door of the house with his nephew at his side. The boy trembled and rubbed his hands together. He knew the court's tales about his mother and feared that she might curse him on the spot. He held his uncle's gaze and wanted desperately to be protected by his magic. They crossed the threshold of the house and met the two women and the maids who sat by the table. Gwydion took in the sight of these fallen women gathered in the house and tried not to sneer. He noted that Goewin hadn't lost her beauty, nor had his sister.

Arianrhod rose and greeted Gwydion. Eight years had passed and nothing much had changed about him. He still wore the same white tunic and brushed his fair locks behind his head. Arianrhod noted the boy's presence and nodded to him. The boy, frozen on the spot, stared at his mother in awe. Arianrhod's eyes narrowed when she saw his lip tremble.

"Gwydion, who is this boy? An apprentice magician?" Arianrhod asked.

"No, Arianrhod. This is your son, born eight years ago in the King's court." Gwydion said.

Arianrhod gripped onto a nearby chair for support. She felt tears swell in her eyes as she took in the young boy in front of her. She remembered the fateful day in a sudden wave and her chest heaved with the same sob that gripped her. Her eyes flickered to Gwydion, who watched her every reaction dispassionately. Arianrhod's heart ached before it raged. No tricks, she'd asked. No tricks.

"You kept him from me after all of this time?" Arianrhod said.

"And now he is here. He needs a name, sister," Gwydion replied. "You are his mother."

"I thought he was dead."

Arianrhod's face crumbled and she looked away from the boy. The shame she had endured on that day came back to her. The embarrassment and disgrace returned, melding the years that separated them. What was worse was how Gwydion had hidden her son to use him against her and remind her of the humiliation all those years ago.

"A name, Arianrhod," Gwydion insisted.

"The boy will never have a name unless it is given to him by me," Arianrhod snapped. The tynged, the fate set in place and Gwydion felt the power of her words shake the house.

Gwydion dug his heels into the floor. This was not how he had expected her to react. The boy stood, dumb and motionless, watching the exchange. Gwydion bit his lip and inclined his head. His head ran away with him as he started concocting a plan that would put an end to this foolish fate.

"So be it. Your son shall be nameless," Gwydion said. He turned on his heel and took the boy with him. Arianrhod kept her head turned away and felt the tears burning her cheeks. When they left, she walked to the window and watched her son disappear.

~

Months passed and Gwydion set about his plan. His nephew didn't know about the finer details but knew that it would involve tricking his mother. The boy remembered the look on his mother's face when he realised who he was. It was etched in his memories, haunting his dreams. He didn't want to trick her, but he had no power to change his uncle's mind. When Gwydion decided on something, it would be so.

The boy went over the plan with his uncle. He practised his stone throwing and tried not to think about how his mother would react. He felt angry for how his mother gave him this fate but felt equally angry that his uncle would continue to treat her so. He agreed to carry out the plan and Gwydion sent the boy to the woods where Arianrhod lived.

After her tynged, Gwydion enchanted the woods to cage Arianrhod from the outside world. She spent her days reading or walking with her lover Goewin. After watching her movements, Gwydion timed the encounter with the boy to perfection. He knew that Arianrhod and Goewin would walk the same path in the woods at that exact point in time. Gwydion hid behind one of the bushes and peered through the leaves. The boy stood, stones dangling from his pockets, to wait for the women to appear on the path.

Walking along the beaten path, Arianrhod and Goewin chattered away. They pointed out certain birds to each other or identified the different species of tree that surrounded them. They often walked barefoot together, revelling in the feel of the earth on their feet. Arianrhod spotted a fair-haired boy playing with stones in the distance. His back was turned away from them and so Arianrhod called to him. The boy, keeping to Gwydion's plan, refused to turn. He threw a stone towards one of the wrens and hit one square on the chest. The wren squawked and flew away in a fit of anger.

"Incredible! The fair-haired one with a skillful hand," Arianrhod clapped. Goewin, on the other hand, scowled at the boy for disturbing the wrens.

From where he had been hiding in the bush, Gwydion jumped out in victory and lifted the boy in his arms. Arianrhod froze beside Goewin and watched her brother pounce on the young boy.

"And he is named! Lleu Llaw Gyffes - the fair-haired one with the skillful hand," Gwydion laughed, but the boy was not laughing with him.

Arianrhod buried her face in her hands and Goewin held her shoulders. Her shoulders shook beneath Goewin's hands and she felt the pain of seeing Gwydion wreak havoc on her body. Arianrhod felt the heat of her crying scald her skin and she held onto Goewin to keep her upright.

"How dare you?" Goewin said to Gwydion. "You and your wretched tricks –"

"Your son is named. Next, he will take up arms and he will soon become a man," Gwydion cheered.

"That boy will never possess arms unless I arm him," Arianrhod yelled in fury.

Gwydion set Lleu down on his feet. The second tynged settled in the air around them. The woods shivered from Arianrhod's words, and the wrens nestled closer together overhead. The magic rippled along her fingertips and she clenched her hands into fists.

Enraged, Gwydion wrapped his cloak around Lleu and they vanished out of sight. Arianrhod mourned for the loss of her son and how her brother continued to use him against her. Goewin led her sobbing body away from the scene and consoled her. She would hold her in the bed they shared and take the flood of tears that came. Arianrhod would wonder whether her brother held her son under some spell. He used him to manipulate her and she dreaded to think what her brother would do next.

Bound to the woods by his spell, Arianrhod was

powerless to stop him. She would have done anything to have retrieved her son from him. Goewin and the maids would send word or try to find Gwydion themselves, but it came to no avail. He escaped their searching and Lleu Llaw Gyffes was under the King's protection. Unless he went himself to Arianrhod's woods, her son was lost to her and Gwydion would continue to pour lies down his throat.

~

It took years for Gwydion to hatch his next plan. Lleu Llaw Gyffes grew into a young man and became renowned for his skills and horsemanship. Gwydion despaired that his nephew would be deprived of weapons because of his sister's tynged. He rejoiced that he was given a name but felt angered that he could not use the weapons that he sorely deserved. Lleu watched as his friends took arms and his mother's tynged stopped him from joining them. Gwydion evaded Goewin's prying into his affairs and ensured Lleu's protection by the Crown. If it took years to arm him, so be it.

Gwydion told Lleu that he would be able to see his mother again. They would need to disguise themselves as bards and visit Arianrhod to ask for lodgings for the night. Lleu listened to his uncle's plan and felt his gut twisting with the memories of his mother. He remembered the tricks they had played on his mother when he was a young boy and he regretted them sorely. For the first time, Lleu put his foot down with his uncle.

"No more tricks," Lleu said to him.

"Don't you want to see your mother again, after so long? Yes, she may have rejected you, but haven't you wondered how she is, what she looks like?" Gwydion said.

Lleu admitted that he had done little else when he thought of her. There wasn't a day that went by when he didn't wonder about his mother Arianrhod. He went so far as to wonder whether she was wondering about him. Gwydion insisted that Arianrhod cared little for him, but from her reactions to his arrival at the cottage, he couldn't have been sure. Gwydion wouldn't allow him to see her alone, nor did Lleu have any idea on how to find her if he wanted to. His only link to his mother was through Gwydion.

"In order to see her, I must disguise myself as a bard?" Lleu asked.

"Precisely. We must act the part and, after spending the night, we will return here. She will be none the wiser," Gwydion asked.

"So, it is a trick," Lleu said.

"She will know nothing of it. I will not taunt her any longer – it is child's play," Gwydion assured him. "You will see her and she will remain unharmed. I know how you care for her. She is your mother and it is natural that you feel this way."

Lleu relented to his uncle's pleas and agreed to disguise himself as a bard with him. Gwydion used his magic to make their disguises as convincing as possible. Lleu felt the familiar feeling from his boyhood of something not being right. He trusted his uncle from his boyhood and that was precisely what made him fear the worst.

Gwydion transported them by his cloak to the woods where Arianrhod lived with Goewin and the maids. Lleu looked around and noticed that not much besides the seasons had changed since he was last there as a young boy. Gwydion led the way along the footpath and Lleu followed closely behind. The same childish fears gripped him as a man just as they did when he was young. He resisted the urge to hold his uncle's hand like he did as a boy.

The house stood in the same spot as it had done all those years ago. The disguise felt heavy on his body and he wanted to see his mother as Lleu, not a bard. Never had this hiraeth, this longing to return to this place felt more potent. Gwydion knocked his hand on the door and Lleu held his breath. Curiosity would always get the better of him, in the end.

Goewin answered the door. She had aged since their last visit, but almost imperceptibly. Her eyes flickered from one bard to the other and she beckoned for Arianrhod to come. A maid set down her dough of bread and held onto a kitchen knife. They could have been thieves for all they knew.

"Who is it, Goewin?" Arianrhod asked.

"We are lost here in these woods. We are bards from Môn searching for lodgings. Would you be so kind as to accommodate us for the night?" Gwydion said.

Not only had Gwydion changed their appearances, but their voices too. Lleu tried not to stare openly at his mother, who stood behind Goewin. Unlike Goewin, age showed itself on her face openly. There were faint lines across her forehead and dark circles underneath her eyes. She seemed much thinner than the last time.

Before Goewin spoke, Arianrhod opened the door wider and let the two bards inside. The maid placed the knife down and carried on kneading the dough on the counter-top. Gwydion, prepared for the role, started to recite some verses and he gesticulated his hands as he spoke. Goewin laughed and urged him to carry on.

"What of the other bard?" Arianrhod asked.

"He is being trained in the arts. He will recite some lines tonight - I assure you," Gwydion said, patting his hand on Lleu's shoulder.

The sky darkened outside and Gwydion opened his satchel. He took out a couple of bottles of mead and set them down on the table. Goewin clapped her hands, overjoyed. Arianrhod raised her eyebrow at the bard.

"You are in no shortage of drink," Arianrhod said.

"What can I say? We are bards," Gwydion chuckled.

They settled into eachothers company and laughed together into the night. Gwydion urged Lleu to recite a few lines and the women clapped when he recited some poetry he learned from his schooling. When they all made their way to bed, Gwydion was alert. Lleu lay down and watched his uncle pace in circles. He stared at the ceiling and felt tears threaten to fall down his cheeks. To have seen his mother had moved him more than he dared to admit.

"Do not hold this against me, Lleu," Gwydion said.

"What?"

Gwydion turned around. He extended out his arms and his palms faced the window. Lleu watched, mouth agape, as his uncle murmured his spells. In the distance, Lleu could hear horses galloping towards the house. Lleu jumped out of his bed and grabbed Gwydion with both hands.

"What have you done? You said no tricks. A disguise and no more," Lleu snapped.

Before Lleu could say more, he could hear the women outside of the bedroom. Arianrhod threw the door open and tugged Lleu and Gwydion out.

"Hurry! Hurry! We're under attack! Arm yourselves!" Arianrhod yelled.

Arianrhod opened a chest and hauled out a couple of swords and shields. She handed Lleu a sword and shield as she dug around the cupboard for more. Gwydion, unable to believe his luck, laughed and raised his arms into the sky. The sound of galloping stopped and Arianrhod stopped too. She had heard that laughter before, long ago. She turned her head and saw Gwydion and Lleu, without their disguises, standing before her.

"You armed him! Now Lleu is a man. Soon, he will marry and have children. Your evil fates will plight him no more," Gwydion roared in victory.

Arianrhod looked at Lleu who held the sword and shield in his two hands. Her eyes flickered to his face and she took in how much her son had grown. He was indeed becoming a man, and it terrified her.

"Mother, I never –" Lleu started.

"Lleu Llaw Gyffes will never have a wife made of flesh," Arianrhod said.

Gwydion could have killed his sister then and there. Lleu's eyes widened as the tynged escaped her lips. Goewin and the maids ran inside and staggered in shock to see Gwydion and Lleu. They now understood why the attack had suddenly ceased.

"You would deprive your son of a wife?" Gwydion raged at her. "You selfish, inconsiderate witch. I should kill you now, with my bare hands –"

"Uncle, it is done," Lleu pulled his uncle away from Arianrhod.

"We are nowhere near done. Mark my words, Arianrhod – you have not succeeded. This boy will have his wife even if it kills me. And I will spare your life now so you may see it."

"Get out!" Goewin yelled.

"With pleasure," Gwydion spat. "And do not think that I am ignorant to your relationship. It is immoral and disgusting."

Gwydion grabbed Lleu's shoulder and they vanished into thin air. Arianrhod didn't have the will to cry. She stared at the spot where her brother and son stood some mere seconds ago. Goewin ran to her and tried to console her. Arianrhod couldn't feel nor hear Goewin in those moments. Severed from reality, she could only see her son's face in front of her. Arianrhod fell to her knees and touched the place where he stood. She then breathed in the same air he once breathed.

~

Gwydion and Lleu landed back in the King's Hall. Lleu fell back onto the ground from the impact and Gwydion stormed over to the King's throne. Lleu chased his uncle and recognised the feeling from how he resented Arianrhod for the tynged. His body shook with rage from his mother's tynged and his face burned with the embarrassment of having trusted his uncle so fully. All the pent-up emotions began to surge through his chest. His hands and arms were shaking and his palms were coated with his own sweat. Gwydion flicked his hand and Lleu felt himself pushed back onto the floor. He staggered from the spell and felt his back thud on the floor. Lleu hauled himself up again and continued to tail his uncle.

"Uncle! Stop this nonsense at once," Lleu snapped.

"I know you are angry, Lleu, but believe you me – there is nobody in Cymru angrier than I am now," Gwydion shouted from the King's Hall.

King Math of Gwynedd heard Gwydion before he saw him. Gwydion kicked open the King's doors and didn't even so much as bow to the King and the virgin footholder. He waved his arms around and explained what had just occurred with his sister Arianrhod. The King listened and became infuriated himself that Arianrhod placed another tynged on the boy. When he heard the nature of the tynged, he frowned and understood Gwydion's rage. Lleu watched the exchange from afar, powerless to intervene.

"Arianrhod is indeed cruel, Gwydion. But do not despair – I have an idea. You said the tynged means that Lleu cannot have a wife made of flesh. Well then, you must fashion a wife for him made from the earth," The King said.

Gwydion admitted that he liked this idea. Lleu walked forward to speak, but Gwydion told him to stay silent for now. The virgin footholder tried not to sigh or even roll her eyes as the men bickered. The King insisted that it would be simple.

"My King, if it is within your power to have the materials gathered – oak, broom and meadowsweet preferably – then I may be able to fashion him a wife out of flowers," Gwydion said.

"It is done. My loyal servants will collect the materials that you need and the boy will have a wife," The King said.

The servants went ahead to collect the oak, broom and meadowsweet at once. It took a day for them to collect the quantities that would satisfy Gwydion, but it was done. The servants, sweating from the exertion, retreated to the kitchens after Gwydion took the buckets from them. He set down the three materials in the King's Hall and Lleu felt the familiar feeling of discomfort enter his stomach. The King grinned when he saw the excitement on his magician's face.

"We will make her now. There is no time to lose!" Gwydion laughed.

Lleu, who now stood by the King's throne, watched his uncle summoning the elements. Gwydion knelt onto the red carpet and raised his arms above his head. Lleu, the King and the footholder could only hear the mumblings and grumblings of a madman at his work. Slowly, the oak, broom and meadowsweet rose from the buckets and came together. They blended in front of Gwydion and started to take shape.

The King gripped the arms of his throne and Lleu closed his eyes from the light that came from the scene. When he opened them again, there was a lady standing in the centre of the hall. She looked like any other lady, besides the abundance of flowers in her hair and across her dress.

"Here she is. Blodeuwedd, a lady made from flowers," Gwydion said.

The footholder almost fainted at the sight. The King's mouth lay open and Lleu held his breath, waiting to see what she would do. She stared at Gwydion and he held out his hand to her. Blodeuwedd took his hand and he led her to Lleu.

"Can she... speak?" Lleu asked his uncle.

"Yes. Here, Blodeuwedd – here is Lleu Llaw Gyffes. He will be your husband."

"Hello, Lleu Llaw Gyffes," Blodeuwedd said.

~

Word reached Arianrhod about Blodeuwedd's creation. Arianrhod was enraged that Gwydion and the King would go so far as to create a wife out of the ground for her son. She felt enraged at herself for having uttered the words in the first place. To have punished her son for the crimes of Gwydion and the King was a mistake. Lleu didn't deserve to suffer because of Gwydion's tricks.

Nobody was angrier at Arianrhod than herself. She felt infuriated that these men had brought out this terrifying darkness within her. Gwydion would not get the better of her now. The men who had slighted, abused, and shunned her would not succeed again.

~

Miles and miles away, Lleu Llaw Gyffes came to know Blodeuwedd. She was quiet and reserved most of the time, besides when they spoke about the flowers in the King's meadows. She piped up and talked about the various species that graced their fields during Spring. Blodeuwedd listened to Lleu when he spoke about his weapons, armoury, and horses, but found that she didn't find much interest in him at all. She started to feel duped by creation for having been made to be his wife. She sensed that he didn't regard her with much interest either. They were worlds apart, but Gwydion insisted that they would marry soon.

Lleu wondered whether the union to Blodeuwedd could be stopped. Neither Lleu nor Blodeuwedd wanted the marriage to go ahead and it seemed that Gwydion was blind to it. Lleu also wondered whether his mother and another tynged could stop it from happening. When Lleu told Gwydion how things stood with Blodeuwedd, he refused to listen.

"What? She is exquisite. She is beautiful – one of the most beautiful women to have graced this earth. What more do you want from a wife?" Gwydion said to him.

"She is wonderful, yes, but I don't think I can marry her," Lleu said.

"You will marry her. I will not pluck another woman out of the earth – I might not be so lucky a second time. You cannot keep taking from the elements and expect a perfect result each time," Gwydion said. "It has been decided. Do not worry, my boy, your feelings will change in time. Once the union is sealed, you will love her dearly."

Blodeuwedd had nobody to confide in about her feelings. She would be struck by Gwydion or even the King if she were to voice her discontent. Silently, she wanted a different life. She felt as though the earth and Gwydion had cheated her out of her own existence. She had been created for Lleu and no more. Could she not live for herself? Blodeuwedd despaired that she had no choice in the matter and desperately wanted to be cut loose from this tynged.

Lleu decided that he needed to act. He wondered what would make Gwydion listen to him. Lleu made his way to the King's Hall and Gwydion eyed him suspiciously when he came in, knelt on one knee, and bowed before the three of them. He shivered and felt the palms of his hands start to sweat profusely.

"Lleu, what brings you away from your wife to be?" The King asked after he bade for Lleu to rise.

"I have a condition to set upon marrying Blodeuwedd that I would like to set to my uncle Gwydion," Lleu said.

"Name it," Gwydion said.

"You must release my mother from her bonds to the woods. She may roam free wherever she wishes."

Gwydion frowned at him. "And why ever would I want to let that woman –"

"You told me to name my condition and I have. Release her," Lleu said.

"She is a danger to you and us all," Gwydion snapped. "The King would say as much –"

"Thank you, Gwydion, but I think differently." The King said. "Arianrhod has served her sentence. Perhaps, if she were released from the magical bonds, she may feel less inclined to place fates on your nephew."

Gwydion's fists were clenched. He knew that the King would have the last word and there was little else he would be able to do about it. Lleu watched his uncle running the idea through his head and hesitating. If unsuccessful, he knew he could plead with the King for his mother's release.

"Release her," Lleu insisted.

Gwydion stared into his nephew's eyes and saw that he wouldn't back down, especially when it came to this. He expected his nephew to have developed a hatred for her over the course of her life, but their separation seemed to have made the bond between mother and son even stronger.

"Very well, Lleu. I will release that pathetic woman from her bonds and you will be married to Blodeuwedd tomorrow," Gwydion said. He wrapped his green cloak around his shoulders and vanished.

~

Arianrhod felt him land in the woods. She was tending the garden and felt the energy of the nearby woods change when he landed. She made her way there, as though summoned by him, and saw him walking towards her in the distance. Arianrhod came to the threshold of where she could not cross. There was a huge barrier, invisible to the naked eye, that shimmered between her and Gwydion. She'd tried touching it years ago and it sent stabbing pains through her arm. She stood, metres away from him, and watched him rolling up his sleeves.

"I heard that you succeeded in making a wife for my son out of the earth," Arianrhod said. "Are you here to boast?"

"No, I am here to release you. It is your son's wish before his wedding, but you are not to attend," Gwydion said. "If you meddle with the union, I will kill you and show no mercy."

Her brother's words sent a chill down Arianrhod's spine. His eyes were wide and his magic floated like daggers around him. He lifted his hands and chanted the spells that would release her. Arianrhod felt the creases on her forehead begin to loosen as Gwydion, line by line, broke her from the bonds that kept her in these woods and away from the world. She knelt to the earth and felt the bliss of freedom wash through her. It felt like touching the land again after being exiled to the sea. When Gwydion finished, she looked up at him. He stared down at her, expressionless, before disappearing.

Arianrhod walked past the threshold and breathed deeply. She felt the wind gather around her and whisper in her ear. She spent a time in the grace of this newfound freedom and greeted the trees that had been out of her reach. The wrens in the trees reminded her of her son, Lleu. She could see him as a boy with his rocks weighing down his pockets. He had asked for her release after all that she had done. In her mind's eye, he skipped in the distance and aimed his stones at the tree trunks.

Arianrhod walked home and wondered how she would see her son again before he married Blodeuwedd. As soon as she told Goewin what had happened, they decided to leave for the King's court. It would go against Gwydion's command, but the drive to see her son again overrode those fears. They travelled into the night on horseback and well into the morning. They stopped only for rest and provisions before continuing their path. They camped for the night in a wood near a lake but slept little. They nestled together for cover until the sun rose and they travelled further north to the court.

~

Preparations were being made for Blodeuwedd's wedding to Lleu. The maids were plaiting her hair and weaving all manner of flowers, leaves and branches into the plaits. Blodeuwedd sat and weaved herself a flower crown. Staring at the crown when she weaved it, she could barely look at herself in the mirror. She sat despondent in her white wedding dress and ignored the maids' comments about her beauty.

"Done!" The maid said. "You look a picture, Blodeuwedd. Lleu will be honoured to have you as his wife."

"Thank you," Blodeuwedd said. "Now, may I be left alone for a few moments? I suppose these will be some of my last minutes of peace for a while."

The maids bowed and left Blodeuwedd in her room. She stood up and paced the room in endless circles. She only stopped her pacing when she heard a noise from outside of her bedroom window. Blodeuwedd stuck her flowered head out of the window and spotted a figure scaling the wall. She staggered back and held her hand to her chest. Her breathing quickened and she held onto one of the posts of the four-poster bed to keep her upright. Blodeuwedd watched as the figure hauled themselves over the windowpane and into the room.

Arianrhod brushed herself off and looked up. Blodeuwedd froze, unable to comprehend why this woman had taken such pains to find her. She looked middle-aged, possibly widowed, and far too old to be scaling stone walls. Blodeuwedd stared at the knife that was sheathed on the belt of her dress and felt the breath in her lungs escape.

"Blodeuwedd," she said. "I am Arianrhod, Lleu's mother."

Arianrhod bowed to her before watching a look of utter shock pass over her face. Blodeuwedd, having heard about the mother's plight, ran to her with open arms and embraced her. Arianrhod held her and moments passed in this silent embrace. She felt tears soak into her shoulder from the young woman and her heart broke. Both women, who had suffered under Gwydion's hands, felt the bond of sacred sisterhood extend to one another, like an invisible thread hooking onto each of their hearts.

Blodeuwedd sent for the maids. Arianrhod stayed hidden when the maids came in and she listened to Blodeuwedd ordering for them to get Lleu to her room. The maids implored her to tell them what was wrong, but she kept the information away in the heart that kept the silent bond between her and Arianrhod.

"Lleu must come here at once. It is a very urgent matter concerning the proceedings of the wedding. It cannot be resolved any other way," Blodeuwedd said.

Arianrhod and Blodeuwedd sat beside one another on the bed and waited for Lleu to arrive. Arianrhod's palms, coated with sweat, held onto Blodeuwedd for support. Her heart pounded in her chest and she wished that Goewin was there to comfort her.

Arianrhod stood up and Blodeuwedd went to answer the door. Lleu stepped in, confused that he had been summoned. He raised his head and thought Blodeuwedd had conjured an apparition.

Arianrhod ran to her son and flung her arms around him. She expected to see Gwydion behind him, but relaxed when she realised her son was alone. They stood in their embrace for what felt like an age and wiped eachothers tears. They were silent, unable to exchange a single word to one another. Blodeuwedd watched them in silence. It took a while for Lleu to think of the words to say to her.

"I am sorry that I did not seek you out. You must understand that my uncle, your brother, made it difficult –"

"I am the one who must apologise," Arianrhod said quickly. "You must know that I regret my actions more than you could ever know."

"But why the name? Why the arms and why the wife?" Lleu asked. It was the question that had been on his mind ever since Blodeuwedd came from the ground.

"It was... foolish. I wanted to deny you the things that would make you a man. Your own name, weapons to carry and a wife," Arianrhod said. "For that I am sorry. I wanted to stop you from becoming like my brother and the King."

Lleu held his mother's hands and forgave her. Now, after all these years, he understood her plight completely. Arianrhod turned her head to Blodeuwedd.

"You are to marry my son?"

Blodeuwedd looked at Lleu, who felt as equally despondent about the situation as she did. She sighed and Lleu kept his head low. Arianrhod looked from Blodeuwedd to her son and realised quickly that they were not, as she assumed, madly in love with one another. This marriage looked like the last thing in the world that they wanted to do.

"It is what Gwydion wants," Blodeuwedd said.

"What is it that you want, Blodeuwedd?" Lleu asked her.

"To be free."

Arianrhod held her hand and they heard movement outside of Blodeuwedd's bedroom door and fear gripped them. The door opened and Arianrhod's suspicions were confirmed when Gwydion stepped foot through the door and into the room. He wore his finest tunic for the wedding and his blonde hair was combed back without a single strand out of place.

"Sister. What a surprise," Gwydion said. He slammed the door shut behind him and shot Lleu an angry glare.

"They don't want this marriage, Gwydion. You are foolish to force it on them," Arianrhod said.

"I think you are the last person to begin calling people fools," Gwydion said. "You should have taken your chance for freedom when I gave it to you. Instead, you have chosen to die."

When Gwydion began his spell, Lleu reached for his sword. Before he managed to take it out, Arianrhod grabbed the knife that was sheathed in the belt of her dress and lunged for Gwydion. She sank the knife into the centre of his chest, aiming for his heart, and stared into the green of his eyes.

Gwydion staggered and Arianrhod shoved the knife further into his chest. His mouth, agape, closed before he plummeted to the floor. Caught off his guard, Arianrhod watched his eyes widen slightly before slackening. Arianrhod pulled the knife from his heart and blood oozed from the wound. The side of his lip began to run red down to the crook of his neck. She moved away from the corpse and dropped the knife to the floor with a clatter.

Lleu stared at Gwydion's lifeless body, expecting the pang of grief to hit his chest. It never came. He watched the blood pooling around the wound near his heart and felt nothing. He raised his eyes to Arianrhod and felt relief for what she had done. Blodeuwedd couldn't speak nor move for shock. Her creator lay motionless on the floor and she suddenly felt free.

They left the King's court and found horses to escape. Finding Goewin hidden away, they stopped for breath. They knew that, soon, Gwydion's body would be found and that they would be the first suspects.

"Go now, my son, my Lleu," Arianrhod said.

"But what will the three of you do?" Lleu asked.

"If Blodeuwedd wishes, she may join us and we will find our freedom," Arianrhod said. "Go now and live your life. Never forget the women who spared you."

"I will see you again."

"That is our tynged. We will see each other again," Arianrhod said.

Lleu held onto his mother's hands and thanked her. When he left on horseback, the three women made their way in the opposite direction. They left behind the court, their homes and everything that they knew. The guards would find Gwydion's body in Blodeuwedd's room and run for the King. They would find that Lleu and Blodeuwedd had gone and the King would assume they left together for freedom from Gwydion's magical clutches. He would be short of a magician and so search the lands for another. They would never know the truth of what happened on that day.

When they left Gwynedd, their hearts soared with the prospect of a new beginning. The flowers in Blodeuwedd's hair fell out of her hair and wedding dress as they rode far, far away. They travelled off the beaten track and into lands where nobody would know them.

Blodeuwedd drank in the new sights like a newborn child and held onto Arianrhod's waist for dear life. Goewin led the way and they decided to keep travelling south. They had faced so many horrors as women and hoped to begin a new life with joy. Arianrhod couldn't think of any life better than living in harmony with the land and with each other.

In the distance, the sun began to rise over the brow of the hill. Blodeuwedd watched the flowers begin to fold open as the light of the sun began to touch their petals. Goewin and Arianrhod held eachothers hands and watched Blodeuwedd, who was overjoyed by the sun's arrival. She rose with the flowers and watched the sun, once peeking over the hill, arrive fully in the sky. Goewin and Arianrhod rose to hold Blodeuwedd's hands and they thanked the sun for another day of freedom.

Olwen

Culhwch, son of King Cilydd, was summoned by his stepmother to discuss his options for taking a wife. He descended the stairs that led to her chambers and ran through what excuses he might conjure to escape her suggestions. Each step felt heavier than the last and he never thought he could quite accept that she slept in the room where his mother once slept. Culhwch resented his father for having married her and made her the new Queen.

The Queen bade for him to enter and Culhwch found her sitting in front of her vanity, her lady-in-waiting behind her. She was brushing the long brown locks that cascaded in waves down her back. Culhwch kept his eyes trained firmly on the floor and he tried to stop himself from fidgeting with his hands, betraying his nerves to her.

"You know why I have summoned you, Culhwch," the Queen said.

"Yes. You wish for me to marry someone at once."

"Not just anyone. You will marry my daughter Eirianwen."

Culhwch's eyes shot up to her at this. His stepsister? The Queen smiled steadily at him and he wanted to pinch himself to wake up from this horrific nightmare. Instead, his fists clenched and his blood pumped with rage.

"No. I will not marry Eirianwen," Culhwch said. "I would sooner die."

The Queen's face contorted into her own anger and she stood up from her chair, making the lady-in-waiting step back hurriedly. She clenched her own fists. She had successfully married the King and she would not stop until her lineage was well and truly royal. The Queen took hurried steps towards him and Culhwch stepped away from her.

"You will marry your stepsister and that is final," said the Queen.

"And what does my father say about this?" Culhwch snapped. "You are not my mother. My mother was and will always be the Lady Goleudydd, alive or dead."

The Queen was furious. She stared into the black of his eyes. She knew very well that Culhwch would not back down and agree to marrying her daughter. The Queen summoned all her pent-up anger and devised, in a matter of moments, a curse that would make him regret what he had done. Nobody, not even this Prince, would stop her from getting what she wanted.

"Very well," she said. "If you refuse to marry Eirianwen, you cannot marry anyone but Olwen, the daughter of the giant Ysbaddaden Pencawr."

"Ridiculous!" Culhwch snapped before leaving the Queen's bed chambers and making his way immediately to his father Cilydd.

Having returned from hunting, the King was unaware of what had transpired between his wife and son. Cilydd could only see an enraged Culhwch making his way over to him and his men. Culhwch waved his arms around as he explained to his father what had just occurred. He also made a point of asking who in all Cymru was this woman called Olwen.

"This is grave indeed, Culhwch," said one of the King's men. "Olwen is the daughter of an almighty giant who will not relinquish her to any man."

"You must get her to revert the curse, father. She has set an impossible task for me!" Culhwch groaned.

"I cannot, Culhwch. A curse is a curse. You must marry Eirianwen," Cilydd replied evenly.

"You would take her side against mine? Your own son?" said Culhwch.

"She is my wife and your Queen," Cilydd said. He refused to rise to the rage that grew in his son. He found himself stuck between his wife and his child.

"My mother was your wife and your Queen!" Culhwch snapped.

In all his raging, Culhwch found himself wondering about Olwen. He had never heard anything about this mysterious woman until he'd angrily inquired every passerby he saw before his father's arrival. She was the woman impossible to attain because her father, the giant, prevented anyone from trying to get to her. Her beauty, he heard, was renowned through the land where she resided.

"Fine," Culhwch spat. "So be it. I will defeat the giant and retrieve Olwen. She will be my wife."

"Wait! Culhwch!" Cilydd yelled, almost unable to believe he would attempt the impossible. "I implore you to go to your cousin Arthur for help in retrieving Olwen. If you have any chance of getting to her, it will be with his help."

~

Culhwch left the following morning and sent word to Arthur, his kinsman, who lived in a place called Celliwig in Cornwall. His father assured him that Arthur was one of the finest men in the land and more than capable of helping him in defeating the giant who guarded Olwen.

Arthur invited Culhwch to his court in Cornwall. He made the long and arduous journey down to the south, becoming more and more determined to obtain Olwen as his wife. He started to believe that, if he succeeded, this curse might become a blessing. If she was indeed the fairest in all the lands, he would have her as his wife. Culhwch's anger at his fate and his strange passion for Olwen goaded him on.

When Culhwch arrived, he entered into Arthur's court. King Arthur and his men welcomed him in as though he were an old friend and not some distant kinsman of whom they'd only heard about by name. He extended out his arms and they embraced before heading to the feast that had been prepared for his arrival. He was exhausted from the weeks it had taken him to get there and felt grateful to have arrived there.

"Come, come! Let us eat first before we take more pressing matters into hand," said Arthur.

Culhwch did not eat a morsel before he detailed his

impossible task to King Arthur and his men. He told them about the wicked curse given to him by his stepmother and how he desired, more than anything else, to obtain Olwen as his wife. It was only when Arthur implored him to eat that he took any food to his lips.

"My father Cilydd advised me to come to you. You are experienced, he said, in dealing with such tasks," Culhwch said.

"I would be glad to help you, Culhwch," he replied. "What I cannot do is give you the sacred sword Caledfwlch. That is mine and mine alone."

"I understand," Culhwch nodded. "What I need is your help and your finest men."

"I will gladly help you and give you my finest men," Arthur said. "Cai, Bedwyr, Gwalchmai and, of course, Gwyn ap Nudd."

Culhwch couldn't quite believe what he was hearing. He knew that Gwyn ap Nudd was the King of the Tylwyth Teg, the fair folk. Their advice and guidance would be invaluable on his quest to find Olwen. The fair folk listened to the rhythm of magic that went unnoticed by mere mortal men and so he bowed to Arthur in gratitude. Perhaps, he thought, there was a chance at obtaining Olwen after all.

"I thank you, Arthur," Culhwch said. "I understand that the cave in which she lives is guarded by her father the giant."

"We will get to her, Culhwch, I promise you," Arthur said.

~

After the feast, Culhwch was taken to a room. He lay awake at night and felt more determined than ever to get to Olwen. The possibility of her becoming his wife was becoming manifest by the hour. He wondered whether the task could truly be impossible if he was accompanied by men who had dared to challenge the impossible.

Preparations were made the following morning to travel to the cave where they believed Olwen lived. It took weeks to travel back and they took each opportunity to set up camp and spend the night on their journey. Culhwch did not want to waste a single hour in any one place, so he urged Arthur and his men northward. Culhwch barely felt the fatigue. His thoughts for Olwen dominated his mind and he was energised by every mention of her name. It was Culhwch who woke Arthur and his men in the morning to ensure that they caught as much daylight as possible in their travels. He woke at dawn and slept as soon as the sun set beyond the hills.

When they finally arrived in the area, Culhwch sent a note to every local to discover as much as he could about Olwen and her whereabouts. He even decided to knock on doors himself and speak directly to them so that he may glean a better picture of what this task might entail. The locals spoke about how many men had perished trying to obtain Olwen, but this did not deter Culhwch in the slightest. They told him that the giant would let her out of the cave to wash herself in a nearby stream.

"You will know you have found the place if white lilies grow there. She is called Olwen because those same white flowers sprout where she walks," said one of the locals.

Gwyn ap Nudd and his fair folk had gone to the forest themselves to see if they could find Olwen. When they returned, they told him that they knew which cave would be the one to contain her. Both the fair folk and the locals combined their knowledge and narrowed their search to one area where they were almost certain they would find Olwen's cave.

Culhwch, Arthur, and his men walked through the forest and towards the cave. Culhwch held his sword and looked around as though the giant himself were about to spring out and attack at any moment. They found white lilies growing in droves by a river and could only guess that they were getting closer. Culhwch's heart thumped in his chest as he bent down to touch the delicate lilies with his fingertips.

In the distance, Culhwch spotted a cave. He told Arthur and his men to keep back while he investigated. Arthur insisted that he went with him, but Culhwch was determined to go. Arthur and his men held back near the cave's entrance and watched Culhwch go with his sword. Arthur grasped onto his kinsman's arm and turned him around to face them.

"You are a fool, Culhwch, to believe that you and that sword could bring down the giant," Arthur said. "Let us come with you. At least I will have my sword, Caledfwlch, to swing at him."

The men followed Culhwch into the cave and they

sank further and further into the darkness. In the distance, they could see a light and they followed the cave towards where the light danced in the tunnel. When they came closer to the light, they heard movement.

~

Olwen threw branches of wood onto the fire and wondered when her father would return to the cave. He had not left her for this long before and she knew it must have been some argument about her being unavailable for marriage. She was tired of hearing about the number of men who had died trying and wished only to have permission to go down to wash by the river. It was the one hour she could spend outside of the cave. Her father's spell on her was strong enough to prevent her from even passing the cave walls without his permission.

Long ago, when Olwen was a child, she would practice her magic by the stream and show the water nymphs what she could do. Her father eventually found out that his daughter was practising magic and he forbade her to do so again. Ysbaddaden Pencawr knew that, if she mastered the art, she may well be able to release herself from her bonds and leave him. Over time, Olwen felt the magic drop from her fingertips and back into the earth from whence it came.

Olwen heard footsteps approaching from the cave's entrance and she felt a splinter enter her hand from the grip she had on her twigs. There were multiple footsteps fast approaching and she wondered how on earth they had managed to come in without her father seeing them.

"Who is it?" Olwen called.

She heard one of the footsteps quickening and her heart started to thump with fear. Did these people mean to harm her? She dropped the twigs onto the stone floor and ran further into the cave. She did not stop for a moment to catch her breath.

"Wait! Wait!" a voice called out from behind her.

Olwen refused to stop but knew that this man was hot on her trail. She fell over a sizeable stone and the man held up his own candle towards her. She lifted herself up from her forearms and turned her head to look at one of the intruders.

From the candlelight, Olwen could make out the man's features and his eyes were opened wide. He was staring at her intently and Olwen wanted to keep running. He certainly looked like he meant her harm. He held out his hand for her, but she came up from the ground herself and took a few steps back from him.

"You must be Olwen," the man said.

"Yes, and you are?" Olwen replied.

"Culhwch. I am here to retrieve you from your father."

It was not as though these words were new to Olwen. She smiled at him steadily and nodded her head. She tried to recall the words she used for all the other men who had told her they would release her from her imprisonment. Olwen felt trapped in this perpetual loop of repeating the same hope of release and, eventually, falling into despair when they failed.

"I thank you, my Lord. You will be the one to release me from my imprisonment?" Olwen asked.

"Yes, I swear it," Culhwch replied.

Olwen felt for this poor man. She had felt for all the other poor men who had sworn they would release Olwen and, as a result, died trying. She could do nothing but nod and thank him, because he was her only hope of escape.

Olwen tried, over the years, to escape from this cave herself. She had failed time and time again and she now resigned to whatever hope came her way. She found refuge in the hours she spent washing by the river in the sunlight and the feel of her white lilies on the ground. She despaired that her father had imprisoned her to a barren cave and not to a riverbank or a lone cottage in the woods. There was nothing in that cave but darkness.

"Why does your father imprison you so, Olwen?" Culhwch asked as they walked towards Arthur and his men.

"He will not relinquish me to any man. He fears that, once I am lost to him, he will be forever alone," Olwen replied.

"I will speak to your father," Culhwch promised her.

Olwen wanted to tell him that there was no use in trying to reason with Ysbaddaden Pencawr. Her father was the most stubborn giant in all the lands and this man would be treated no different to all the previous men. She followed him to where Arthur and his men were standing with their weapons in hand.

"We believe Ysbaddaden Pencawr may be – " Arthur started.

A great roar came from the entrance of the cave. Olwen knew the sound and readied herself for the large hand that would follow and grab them all from the inside. She ran to the sides of the cave and watched with a vague sense of guilt as the other men were hauled out by the giant. She ran to the entrance of the cave and found her father staring down at the men with rage.

"Ysbaddaden Pencawr! I am here to ask for your daughter Olwen's hand in marriage," yelled Culhwch.

"Oh, you are?" the giant laughed. "You are a fool, then. The only way you can marry my daughter is by completing forty tasks."

"Name them," Culhwch said. "I will make it my life's work to complete each and every one."

Olwen tried her best not to sigh audibly as her father relayed the forty tasks in detail. She found her eyes starting to shut and a snore building up in her chest. She opened her eyes with a start and found that her father was detailing the thirtieth task. One of the men beside Culhwch was writing everything down on a piece of parchment and Culhwch was committing every single detail to memory. When her father came to the last task, Olwen thanked the heavens that he'd almost finished.

"And do you think, Culhwch son of Cilydd, you can really complete all those tasks?" the giant laughed.

"For Olwen, I will," he said.

Olwen stared at the man with curiosity. She then turned her eyes to watch her father's reaction. He frowned at him and she wondered whether he would be able to restrain himself from killing the man on the spot. She'd seen him done it before and did not doubt that he would do it again. Culhwch bowed to her but she didn't dare, in front of her father, acknowledge his gesture.

Olwen watched Culhwch and his men leaving the cave and she turned to her father. He was suppressing a laugh that threatened to explode into a loud roar. He watched the men retreating with a grin and Olwen tried her best to keep her face as neutral as possible. She, however, held onto the glimmers of hope that she saw in those men's eyes and the determination they cradled in their hands. Without those glimmers of hope, what reason did she have to live?

~

Culhwch and his men wasted no time trying to complete the series of forty tasks set by Ysbaddaden Pencawr. Among them, he had to retrieve the basket of Gwyddneu Garanhir and hunt for Twrch Trwyth, the magical wild boar. Some tasks, they realised, would be easier than others and resolved to complete those first.

Culhwch, in each task, kept the image of Olwen's face in his mind as fresh as the day he'd first laid eyes on her. There wasn't an hour in the day that went by without him thinking about her and imagining her as his wife. He was utterly enchanted by her beauty. She was extremely pale and drawn from the years she'd spent in the hole that was her cave, but in Culhwch's eyes she didn't have a single flaw.

Arthur and his men helped Culhwch in the tasks and ended up risking their lives to complete them. They steeled themselves for whatever came their way and kept the following tasks fresh and ready in their minds. Arthur relished every moment of completing them and became as eager as Culhwch to move on to the next one. He had been waiting for years to face another challenge and, when Culhwch arrived with his tale of woe, he couldn't believe his luck.

"The hunt for the wild boar is among the last," said Arthur.

"How will we catch him?" asked Culhwch.

"There must be something that will prevent him from evading our capture," replied Arthur. "Everything on this world has a weakness."

"We should speak to Gwyn ap Nudd, Lord of the Fair Folk. He may know where the boar's weakness lies."

Gwyn ap Nudd was summoned along with some of the fair folk of the forest and he was questioned about the infamous wild boar. The fair folk sat in a circle around the men and chattered amongst themselves about how the boar might be captured, but to no avail. The boar was wild and his magic was different to the one practiced by the fair folk. Twrch Trwyth could only be seen for seconds before dashing off into the next stretch of woods.

"Does the boar not stop to eat?" Arthur asked Gwyn.

"He must! How else would the creature live?" Culhwch asked.

"We will do our best to watch him," said Gwyn ap Nudd. "We may be able to find out where he stops."

Culhwch decided to go with the fair folk and camp

around the areas where the boar might be spotted. He changed his appearance completely and walked among the fair folk as though he were one himself. Culhwch set up camp and waited for weeks before he finally caught a sighting of what he believed to be Twrch Trwyth.

"There!" Culhwch whispered as he watched the boar dash like a bolt of lightning through the woods. He got up from where he hid and ran towards the place where the boar ran through. He touched the ground and the grass was almost gone from the speed at which the boar tore across the land. The land was warm to the touch and he looked around. The boar was gone in an instant.

Culhwch held onto the hope that the boar might pass through again. Along with the help of the fair folk, he created a trap that might hold Twrch Trwyth. He worked, day and night, on the trap and hoped that more news would arrive about the boar. The fair folk discovered that the boar, when passing through, stripped the bushes of their berries before making his way onto the next feast. Culhwch soaked in every morsel of information and made sure to go about collecting berries for the trap.

Another few weeks passed until the fair folk reported a sighting. The boar had passed through a patch of wood that was adjacent to them and missed the trap completely. Culhwch tried not to despair and instead decided that more traps must be made. He set about working with more of the fair folk to create these traps and scatter them across the woods. There was a chance that the boar might stumble on at least one of them if he passed through again.

"Are you certain that it will work?" Culhwch asked one of the fair folk.

"Yes, it must. There is no other way for us to catch the boar," they replied.

It was only when Culhwch marked the third month of waiting that he saw success. He laid out a huge basket of berries near the trap and knew that the boar wouldn't be able to resist the feast before him. He watched and saw, perhaps for the first and only time, the boar stop beside the basket. He devoured the contents and the trap fell and snapped shut around him.

Culhwch jumped out of where he hid and heard Twrch Trwyth squealing in terror. He sent a messenger to the fair folk and they all confirmed that he'd finally succeeded to capture the wild boar. He took the evidence to Arthur and his men, who themselves had been working on the other tasks that they'd needed to complete for the giant.

"If you have the boar and we have the basket, then we have completed all forty of the giant's tasks," laughed Arthur.

The men rejoiced in wonder and made their way to Olwen's cave at once. They sang songs and took along the evidence of completing each task with them. Culhwch could feel that, with each step, he was walking nearer and nearer to his marriage to Olwen. It would only be a matter of time before they were finally wedded to one another.

It was their singing that caught Olwen's ears first. Their low voices and laughing rang through the forest and Olwen made her way to the cave's entrance. She had already been by the river that morning to wash. The peace of the forest was well and truly shaken by the arrival of these men. The birds sprang out of the trees and the rabbits ran out of their holes. The men pounded the earth with their feet and filled the air with their singing.

Olwen heard her father waking from his slumber and the earth began to move with him. She stood beside the cave's entrance and listened to the men approaching. Olwen dared to hope that they'd been successful and allowed herself to smile. Had that mere mortal man succeeded in those forty tasks? Culhwch, son of Cilydd? Olwen sat on the edge of where the spell prevented her from going and waited for the men to reach her. She waited to hear what they would say to her father.

"As you can see, Ysbaddaden Pencawr, I have completed all the tasks you have set for me," Culhwch yelled. "You must uphold your half of the bargain."

The giant couldn't believe what he was seeing. The swords, the boar and all the evidence of their success lay in huge troves for all to see. He couldn't believe that this mere mortal and his men could ever have been capable of completing the tasks he had set out. He had started getting nervous after hearing word that they completed the thirtieth task.

"I will be married to Olwen at once," said Culhwch.

"You will never marry my daughter," the giant replied. "I would sooner die."

Culhwch had not wanted to force the giant to keep his side of the agreement. He took out a bow and began to aim a poisoned arrow towards the giant. Ysbaddaden Pencawr simply laughed that the mortal thought a small arrow would be enough to kill him. He was laughing when Culhwch shot the poisoned arrow and it pierced one of his eyes.

The giant staggered and Olwen watched in disbelief as her father started to fall. The poisoned arrow sank deep into his socket and his laughing stopped when his body landed with a thud on the ground. Ysbaddaden Pencawr lay dead on the ground and the men began to cheer.

Olwen tried walking beyond the cave walls and she found that she could do so freely. She whispered some of the old spells she had practised as a child and felt the magic calling her home. It gathered around the flesh of her fingers and she raised her hands to the sky. The sun blazed down on her hands and she felt renewed by her freedom. Olwen began walking away from the scene as Culhwch and the men gathered around the dead giant.

"Where is Olwen?" he asked at once.

Olwen heard him say those words as she made her way through the woods. She broke into a sprint and the lilies were growing frantically behind her. She was leaving a trail that sprouted in spirals along the forest path and she had no power to hide the evidence. She could feel her magic returning strongly to her fingertips and she wondered whether she might be able to conceal the lilies with a spell.

"Olwen? Olwen! Your father is dead! We are free to marry, my love," Culhwch yelled.

Olwen could feel that he was close behind and she started running faster. She felt that she should stop to thank him for releasing her but she knew the reason he wanted her. If she stopped to thank him, she would be his wife in minutes. She would be trapped again after having only gained her freedom.

"Olwen?" Culhwch shouted.

Culhwch caught up with her after following the trail of white lilies that betrayed her along the forest path. Some of the flowers were beginning to bloom and others were just pushing through the earth. Exhausted, Olwen slowed her running into a jog. She raised her hands desperately to the sun and begged for the energy to escape her fate. Culhwch caught up with her with a huge grin on his face.

"Thank you for freeing me, but I will not marry you,"

said Olwen.

"What do you mean you will not marry me? Do you not realise the lengths I have gone to secure your hand?" Culhwch said.

"Yes, it must have been exhausting," Olwen frowned. "Why not revel in your successes and then return home to rest?"

"The reason I went to those lengths was to marry you. My stepmother has cursed me to marry nobody but you," Culhwch said.

"A curse indeed," Olwen said. "I must thank you for releasing me, from the bottom of my heart, but I cannot marry you."

"And why-ever not?" Culhwch asked in disbelief.

"Because I am finally free and intend to remain so for the rest of my life," Olwen replied.

She turned away from him and kept walking. White lilies continued to spring from the earth beneath her feet and Culhwch started to trample them in pursuit of her. As she rested from her running, she could feel her energy returning to her and the magic started to pulsate around her fingers again. She knew that she would have to do something if he did not back down.

"You must marry me," Culhwch snapped.

"Culhwch. Is that how you were named? You are indeed narrow. I am under no obligation to marry anyone unless I so wish," Olwen said. "I don't know who you are nor what you are like..."

"You would still be in that cave were it not for me!" Culhwch said. "Does that not tell you enough about who I am and what I am like?"

"Again, I thank you, Lord, for your great kindness to me," Olwen replied. "But I must be on my way."

"Olwen... I am in love with you," said Culhwch.

Culhwch grasped onto her wrist and she jolted back from the force. Olwen turned her head around and Culhwch, insistent, held her wrists firmly with his two hands. He sensed a flicker of fear cross over her features and he let go of her at once. The fantasy that he had built around her was quickly beginning to run through his fingers like sand.

Olwen rubbed her wrists instinctively before moving her hands to Culhwch's cheeks. Her hands were warm like the sun's rays against his face. He closed his eyes and Olwen pressed her hands firmly into his cheeks. She prayed to her fore-mothers that the spell might

71

work. Olwen felt the muscles of his cheeks begin to loosen under her touch and she felt him beginning to fall into her body.

Olwen lay his body down on the floor and felt his chest rise and fall against her. Culhwch lay among the white lilies that were starting to sprout around his body and Olwen planted a kiss on his forehead. She apologised to him and thanked him again before she took his horse and provisions. Olwen hoped that Culhwch would not resent her after he awoke from his slumber. She shed some tears as she went and grieved for all she had lost to gain her freedom.

Culhwch continued to sleep there on the ground for the next few hours. It was Arthur and his men who found him sleeping in the middle of the lilies and jerked him awake. They had released Twrch Trwyth back into the woods as Culhwch searched for Olwen. Twrch Trwyth had bolted from his cage and roamed the woods freely again. Arthur poured a bucket of water over Culhwch's head and he jumped out of the deep sleep he'd been put under.

"What on earth is the matter with you?" Arthur asked. "Where is your horse? Where are the provisions?"

"Olwen. It was Olwen," said Culhwch. "She was here, I swear it."

Culhwch, Arthur and his men searched far and wide for Olwen but she was already gone. They called out her name into the woods and ended up taking their horses to try and follow the many paths she might have taken. There were no white lilies to lead their way and so they could only guess which direction she might have gone.

~

Olwen rode Culhwch's horse deeper into the forest. She felt her magic returning to her and the old spells began to come back to her mind. She even saw Twrch Trwyth whizzing by her and stripping the nearby bushes of their berries and insects. Olwen did not know where she would go but she knew these paths led somewhere. She was now in search of that somewhere.

As she rode further, Olwen watched in awe as the sun began to cast her gold light over the path. The trees and bushes were covered in the gold light of the sun's rays and she rode the horse further through the world of colour that met her. The sun peered through the gaps in the trees and Olwen, once drowned in darkness, lifted her face into the light.

Glossary:

Cymru: Wales
Cymry: Welsh
Caer: Fortress
Éire: Ireland
Éireannach: Irish
Hiraeth: a deep longing for home

A Brief Guide to Pronounciation

Cymru: Come-ruh
Eire: Air-uh
Pwyll: Poo-ee-'ll'*
Alaw: Ah-lah-oo
Matholwch: Mah-th-ohl-oo-'ch'**
Arianrhod: Ah-ree-an-rhod
Goewin: Go-win
Olwen: Ohl-wen
Culhwch: Kill-oo-'ch'**

* In Welsh, the 'll' sound is notoriously difficult for non-native speakers of the Welsh language. Try placing your tongue behind your front teeth and prepare yourself to say 'L'. But, instead of saying 'L', keep your tongue behind your front teeth and blow air out of both sides of your mouth. I would recommend listening to a native speaker pronouncing it, either face-to-face or on a video.

** The 'ch' sound is like how you might say the Scottish word 'Loch'.

Printed in Great Britain
by Amazon